# WENDIGO CHRONICLES

## ENCOUNTERS WITH EVIL

## ERIK LAKE

FREE REIGN
Publishing

ISBN 13: 979-8-89234-036-6

Free Reign Publishing, LLC
San Diego, CA

# CONTENTS

# PREFACE

What is a Wendigo?

A Wendigo is a mythical creature or spirit from the folklore of the Algonquian-speaking peoples of North America. This legend is particularly associated with the Northern forests of the Great Lakes region and the Atlantic Coast. The Wendigo is often described as a malevolent, cannibalistic, supernatural being.

Here are some key aspects of the Wendigo legend:

1. The Wendigo is often depicted as a monstrous creature with some human-like characteristics. Descriptions vary, but common traits include a gaunt, emaciated appearance, symbolizing starvation. Some accounts describe it as a giant, far larger than human beings.

2. The Wendigo is commonly associated with the winter, coldness, famine, and starvation. It symbolizes insatiable greed and excessive consumption, often serving as a metaphor for gluttony and the dangers of overindulgence or greed.

3. A prevalent theme in Wendigo mythology is the transformation of a human into a Wendigo. This transformation could occur if a person resorts to cannibalism or, in some stories, through the influence of a malevolent spirit or during times of extreme physical and emotional distress.

4. The Wendigo myth served as a method of social control, providing a deterrent against cannibalism during times of scarcity. In some narratives, it also reflects the complex relationship between humans and the natural world, emphasizing the importance of balance and respect.

5. The Wendigo has been featured in various aspects of popular culture, including literature, films, and video games. It is often used in horror and fantasy genres, where its frightening characteristics are emphasized.

The Wendigo, as a part of folklore, is not just a simple monster story but a complex narrative that carries significant cultural and moral meanings for the communities that originated the myth.

# INTRODUCTION

Welcome, dear reader, to the spine-tingling pages of *Wendigo Chronicles: Encounters with Evil.* As you embark on this journey, be prepared to enter a world where the line between myth and reality blurs, where the chill of the unknown grips the soul, and where the most primal fears of humanity come to life.

Having ventured through the shadowed forests in *Beyond the Path* and unraveled the enigmatic mysteries in *Things in the Woods*, I've always been fascinated by the darker corners of our world – the places where legends live and breathe. The Wendigo, a haunting embodiment of hunger and horror, has lingered in the whispers of North American folklore for centuries. It's a creature that has always fascinated and terrified me in equal measure.

In *Wendigo Chronicles*, I've gathered a collection of

harrowing tales, each a personal encounter with this chilling legend. These stories are not mere fiction; they are confessions, experiences shared by those who have felt the icy touch of fear, who have looked into the abyss and found something staring back. From the frozen depths of northern forests to the eerie stillness of abandoned towns, each narrative takes you closer to understanding the true essence of this ancient evil.

This anthology is an exploration of our deepest fears – of insatiable hunger, of losing ourselves to something unspeakable, and of the wild, untamed darkness that lurks just beyond the safety of our firelight. The Wendigo is more than a creature; it's a mirror reflecting our own potential for darkness and despair.

So, I invite you to join me. Curl up by the fire, but keep the lights on. Let each story envelop you in its chilling embrace. Remember, while these tales spring from the well of folklore, they carry truths that resonate deep within our bones – truths about survival, the human spirit, and the thin veil that separates us from the unimaginable.

Welcome to the *Wendigo Chronicles*. The journey you're about to undertake is not for the faint of heart. But for those brave enough to face the darkness, a world of eerie wonder awaits.

With a chill in my heart,

Erik Lake

# STORY 1

I grew up in Pennsylvania in the seventies and while we all heard about bigfoot, it really didn't mean much to anyone I knew, one way or another. I mean that in the nicest way possible. It's just something we all would hear people talking about every now and then and we would smile politely and listen, or we would see something on television that looked interesting that might've mentioned bigfoot, but it didn't affect us in our everyday lives. It wasn't until recently that bigfoot has become such a giant phenomenon and back then it was more of a legend that "strange people" believed in, at least as far as my family and I were concerned. I lived in a small, old mining town surrounded by woods and in the middle almost of a very dense and sometimes foreboding forest. There were a few times someone from the town would report having seen or heard something strange in the forest or in the woods otherwise, but no one ever named it as bigfoot or anything else. Even when such reports were put in the local newspaper, and oftentimes they were, it would be on the final page and take up only a paragraph and still no one would want to label whatever it was the witness claimed to have seen. I really wish that things had been a little different and that I was at least taught that those creatures were real, so that maybe I would have had more respect for the wilderness and everything that lived in it. I was so used to blowing off strange things I would see and hear, even in my own backyards or the woods that surrounded it, that it never occurred to me that any of it could happen to me because I thought it could never have happened in the first place. Even when it came to people my family knew well who claimed they saw some sort of strange creature roaming around or heard something devilish out there, we didn't ask questions and my parents told me that they must have either been mistaken or watching too much television. Now that you have the picture of how I was raised involving strange creatures and things in the woods, let me tell you, my story.

Bigfoot was the only known creature and like I said even it wasn't really taken too seriously. I never considered there were other things out there, perhaps scarier, or more deadly than bigfoot, and there were many nights I stayed put and probably kept myself in a dangerous situation because I didn't even flee because I wasn't aware there was anything to worry about. I look back now and think about how delusional everyone must have been to be ignoring all the evidence right in front of them that not only bigfoot, but other creatures were and without a doubt lurking around out there. Once I had this encounter I became almost obsessed with finding answers and when I went to the library for the newspaper archives, I couldn't believe not only how many people had come forward saying they saw bigfoot or other things they couldn't name but that they knew weren't natural to the woods or otherwise didn't belong, but how closely it was happening to where I lived, played and camped all the time. My encounter with one of the most terrifying creatures I have ever seen in my entire life, and that includes in the pages of the horror stories I've read all my life and all the scary movies I've watched combined, when I was on a camping trip at the age of twelve. I was with my two best friends, and we were in the forest that basically surrounded our town. We had been camping out there for as long as I could remember and while it started with us being under the supervision of our dads, we were considered old enough to be out there alone by the time we were ten. We knew what we were doing, and we were a twenty-minute hike in any direction from the safety of someone's home we knew, whichever way we went. We felt safe, we were unarmed, and we were unsuspecting kids. I feel now like we were prime meat for the monster that stalked us that night.

We built a fire and set up our sleeping bags. We didn't use tents because it would have been a lot to carry, along with our food, our books and whatever else we thought we needed out there. We also liked to lay out in the fresh air and look at the sky. All three of us were interested in science fiction and at the time that genre was more filled with aliens from other planets than it is today. Back then though, it was all just a fantasy. We hadn't noticed anything strange and after eating and hanging out for a little while, it was only nine o'clock. We wanted to go for a walk to a clearing in the area where we knew we would be able to get a better look at the stars and the moon, which was full that night. There was too much coverage from all the trees where our little camp was for us to be able to really see it. We all had a set of binoculars but no telescope. There was a clearing that stood on a large hill, or cliff, and we could look down to the tops of the trees below. We felt like kings among men, but our little fantasy was about to be blasted with a large, heaping dose of reality. We started walking the half of a mile or so to the clearing/cliff. We were goofing around and talking but then one of my friends got serious suddenly and told us to be quiet. He asked us if we heard anything but none of us did, we didn't hear anything. That's when it dawned on us that we had a problem. The woods have certain noises about them at night and we weren't hearing anything and in fact it was so quiet that I could hear my own heartbeat and knew if someone had dropped a pin it would have been very audible. We all looked around but when we didn't see anything we stood perfectly still for a moment and that's when we heard what sounded like something walking around where we were standing. We all just looked at one another and silently passed a message to start walking again and to do it at a faster pace than we had originally been moving at. We started to walk but once again knew something was terribly wrong.

There were dead birds everywhere. Once we got to a certain point, almost exactly where we had all stopped to listen, we saw dead birds all over the place. They weren't in piles or anything like that, but we had to be mindful and careful of each step that we took to make sure we didn't step on any of them. There were all different kinds of birds and birds of all different sizes too. We saw at least two owls, but we didn't stick around that area to try and examine how they had been killed or what could have possibly been the perpetrator. We were scared but as young boys we were reluctant to admit it to one another. We kept walking quickly towards the clearing, all the while knowing with absolute certainty that something or someone was following closely behind us. It stopped every time we stopped, and we didn't hear it anymore, but we knew it was there, nonetheless. We could feel it and we knew we had encroached on something's territory that didn't want us there. The constant and inescapable feeling of being watched was almost overwhelming and every minute or two, the foul and rotten stench of decay and filth would waft through the air and across our noses. It was horrible and we would stop and try to catch our breaths, which was impossible to do without tasting the smell. It was repugnant, pungent and vomit inducing to say the very least about it. None of us said it out loud but I think we all considered at one point or another just running for our lives and making our way out of the woods. However, none of us wanted to be the one to suggest it and so we just kept on going.

Suddenly the sound of something whispering our names, one after the other, came right at us. It was coming from behind us but was also, somehow, echoing throughout the entire area. We stopped again and this time the terror was palpable and undeniable. We looked around frantically but still didn't see anyone or anything out there with us. Then the voice changed, and it was almost like whoever was calling us was somehow gaining power. The voice called each of our names in a very bizarre, raspy, and animalistic tone of one of our closest family members. For me it was a badly imperson-ated version of my mother's voice, for one friend his little sister and the other, his grandfather. One by one and at least three times, the voice called out from some-where close to each of us in the stolen voices of our most cherished loved ones. Chills ran up and down our spines and without another word from any of us, we all turned and took off running back to the campsite. We weren't quite ready to give up, but we weren't about to start wandering the woods again. We made it back to the camp safely, but we felt like we had been followed and an awful stench kept wafting around us. We all laid in our sleeping bags and pretended to try and go to sleep. The sun wouldn't come up fast enough and we knew we were getting the hell out of there at first light. However, the beast wasn't done with us yet.

Pretending to sleep worked and we all eventually fell

out. I woke up to that terrible odor and my mother's voice calling me again. This time it was clearer and had much more force behind it. If it had started calling me like this earlier, I would've jumped up and run towards it because it sounded exactly like my mom. But I knew better and hadn't forgotten what had just happened to us only two hours earlier. It was the middle of the night, and I was terrified. I looked all around me and that's when I saw it. The moonlight lit it perfectly. It was twelve feet tall, and so emaciated that it looked like someone had stretched gray and dirty looking skin around each bone. Its ribs stuck out so far, the look of it made me want to puke. It's complexion, that terrible ashen gray color was like the color of death itself and the thing stunk to high heaven. I knew immediately that it was the thing that had been following us all night long just by the smell of it. I wanted to scream and wake my friends up, but nothing would come out. It just stood there, staring at me with its skeleton face and cold, dead, black eyes. It literally looked like it had just crawled out of a grave and its lips were gaunt and bloodied. It dawned on me just then that this had also been the thing that had eaten the poor birds. It stood on two legs and its body and bones looked somewhat human, but it had large antlers, like those you would see on a buck, coming out of its head. There was something about it that was suddenly interesting to me, and I heard a voice in my head telling me to go to it. I started to stand up and one of my friends screamed at the top of his lungs, breaking me free from my strange trance and effectively waking up my other friend as well, who also let out a blood curdling scream at the sight of the monster.

It didn't fly away or speed off into the woods. It slowly stepped backwards and blended back into the darkness of the forest again. We all ran the other way as fast as we could until we reached someone's house that we knew. We pounded down the door. We were crying and terrified, crazed young men who had just had the shock of their lives. The woman who answered ushered us inside and asked a ton of questions before calling each one of our homes. Our parents all showed up together and took us home to our respective houses. We didn't camp again for years but once we did, I became obsessed with finding the beast again. I was never able to but with the invention of the internet and search engines, I feel like I would be prepared if I ever were to come across one again. It was the wendigo, and it would have killed us. I thank my lucky stars that we made it out alive that night and maybe next time I won't be so lucky but I can't help but feel like he and I have some unfinished business and I say "him" because, after all the research I've done and all the information I've come across in the years since this happened to me, I am absolutely sure there was a human man underneath there somewhere, but that he had been under the curse for so long, he had no humanity left in him. Thanks for allowing me to get this out there finally.

# STORY 2

In late fall of 2010, a trek deep into the northern Canadian wilderness took place, involving myself, my father, and my elder brother. Our mission was to hunt moose. Setting off in the early hours, just as dawn broke, we aimed to maximize our travel distance before the approach of night.

Navigating the winding rivers, the day was spent

portaging over challenging rapids. Eventually, we set up our campsite, having made it a little over halfway to where we were headed. My father estimated we'd reach our destination by the next day.

As night enveloped our camp, I ventured out to collect some firewood and headed towards the river-bank, just beyond the warmth and light of our campfire.

It was then, from about 15 yards away in the treeline, that I heard rustling sounds from the bushes. Fixing my eyes on the source of the noise, I suddenly felt a wave of dizziness, accompanied by a foul stench reminiscent of spoiled milk or rotting food. The trees began to subtly shift, taking on the form of a head with faint facial features.

As my eyes adjusted to the dark, a voice emerged from the treeline, eerily familiar – it resembled a relative who had passed away not long ago. The apparition formed into the face of my relative, greeting me with a "Hello" and a plea to come closer. Drawn in but cautious, I stepped forward, only to halt as the situa-tion's strangeness dawned on me. The smiling face of my relative transformed, losing all emotion. The skin paled and started to peel away, with chunks of flesh dropping off their cheeks, sending a jolt of shock and fear through me.

Realizing the danger, I began to retreat towards the camp, noticing too late that I had been unconsciously moving towards the voice, away from the safety of the firelight.

The voice, now angry, shouted for me to come back. As I turned to flee, a glance back revealed a horrifying sight: rotting flesh, gnawed bones, sunken eyes, and a hollow chest - a grotesque, emaciated humanoid figure.

Panic set in as I ran, my voice barely a whisper due to fear. Racing along the riverbank, I could hear the creature's heavy breaths and thudding steps close behind. Reaching the top of the bank, it grasped my leg. Desperately clawing at the ground, I screamed for help, and finally, my voice returned, shouting that something had grabbed me. My brother, awakened by my cries, rushed over, pulling me to safety by the fire.

I was frantic, attempting to describe the nightmarish encounter that resembled, yet so grotesquely differed from, our deceased relative. My brother's solemn nod, confirming his own sighting, solidified the chilling reality of our experience. We spent the rest of the night vigilant, rifles at the ready, and left at dawn without looking back.

The incident left me haunted, plagued by nightmares and unable to sleep for months. Dark figures seemed to peer into my windows, and whispers followed me on nocturnal walks. The daily sightings of a dark figure led me to seek help from shamans, but their ceremonies offered only temporary relief. Friends provided various talismans, from protection pouches to crystals, in their attempts to help.

Research and local lore suggested a harrowing possibility: an encounter with a "wendigo." Surviving such an encounter meant it had latched onto me, parasitically, a connection made possible by its physical touch. Ever since, a sense of dread accompanies me into any forest, a stark contrast to my once cherished outdoor ventures. Now, in the wild, I find myself constantly seeking the safety of a guarded back, forever changed by that fateful night in the northern Canadian wilderness.

# STORY 3

The icy wind stung my cheeks as I trudged through the endless spruce trees, laden with my heavy snowshoes and pack. I had been hiking for hours, with no destination in mind other than away from my troubles back home. Out here in the barren, snow-swept wilderness of northern Canada, I hoped to clear my head and regain perspective, even if just for a few weeks in solitude. I never imagined stumbling into a deeper terror.

I decided to make camp just before dusk in a small clearing with some deadfall for firewood. As I set up my tent, beneath endless darkening skies, I couldn't escape the gut feeling of being watched. Naively I shrugged it off as paranoia from the isolation. The eerie shriek of frigid wind through bare branches certainly didn't help my nerves. Once settled in my tent with freeze-dried beef stew simmering over my camp stove, fatigue quickly set in after a long day of hiking.

I dreamt of being stranded in a dead forest shrouded in mist, while a chorus of anguished screams echoed around me. The horrific shrieks jolted me awake to find those nightmare cries were real! My blood turned to ice as I crawled from my tent, grasping a small hatchet I carried for protection from wildlife. Through the swirling snow and dim moonlight, I made out hulking, skeletal figures – perhaps eight feet tall – bounding on all fours around the edges of my camp. Their ghastly howls pierced my soul, while their glowing red eyes stared through me as they circled closer from the darkness. What godforsaken beasts had I awoken in this forsaken place?

Paralyzed in horror, I tripped over a branch and my hatchet slipped from my icy grip. That's when five of the creatures leapt into the firelight. Gray, leathery skin stretched over their misshapen skeletal bodies like emaciated mummies. Sharp horns curved from their heads above their glowing eyes and fearsome maws filled with yellow fangs. Their skeletal hands and feet ended in talons that clacked on bone as they moved. One towered over me and released an earsplitting shriek as an icy tendril slithered up my spine...a Wendigo! Legends had become flesh!

The Wendigo's breath reeked of decay as it leaned inches from my face, extending a grotesquely long tongue dripping saliva as it sized me up. A hunter sizing up prey. I turned to run but the talons of two more slashed me to the snow. The blood trickling down my back seemed to drive the Wendigos mad with hunger! They retreated several feet and began circling at a distance. I prayed the legends of Wendigos turning men to cannibals with a single bite were untrue, though this dreamlike nightmare made me question all logic.

In a moment of sheer adrenaline, I gained my feet and snatched my hatchet. Its pitted blade and splintered handle seemed so laughably useless now...yet it was all I had between me and being torn apart by these mythical monsters. I knew I couldn't survive long against half a dozen Wendigos, yet my survival instinct forced me to make a stand nonetheless. "Come on then you ugly wretches! I won't die easy!" I shouted in a final act of defiance. My cry seemed to give the beasts momentary pause.

Emboldened, I charged swinging my hatchet wildly while unleashing a barbaric scream. Perhaps the sudden movement triggered their predatory instincts. In a blur of movement my hatchet was torn from my hands as viciously sharp talons slashed into my side. Another flash of searing pain exploded across my back. The snow-covered ground rushed up to meet me as strength drained from my body.

Through dimming vision I saw the smaller Wendigo that scratched me rear back its head, unleashing an earsplitting cry that echoed for miles across the icy wilderness. Soon answering shrieks and howls rang out from every direction. My blood went colder than the frigid air. More were coming. The Wendigos gathering around me clicked their fangs together as they drooled in anticipation of the coming feast.

In those dire moments, I stared down the yawning abyss of my own gruesome demise. Yet through the darkness a tiny light emerged – fiery dawn's first rays peeking over the eastern horizon that begins even in the depths of endless night. And with those heavenly rays came a miracle, as the Wendigos retreated from the clearing, disappearing between the skeletal spruce boughs amidst a cacophony of disappointed howls.

Every labored breath was agony, my shredded

clothing already staining crimson. I couldn't fathom why the beasts had fled. But I knew such demonic creatures would return with reinforcements once daylight fully broke. This was my only chance to escape. Ignoring searing pain I crawled desperately to my tent and retrieved what little I could salvage before this temporary dawn refuge of demons expired. Every minute I expected to hear shrieks announcing the monsters' return. With sheer adrenaline-fueled determination I staggered mile after tortuous mile over the endless snow. I dared not sleep nor rest for two full days and nights until I emerged from those damned woods.

I took it as divine intervention, being given a second chance I scarcely deserved. Since then I have told no one of my ordeal nor sought to verify its reality, wishing to leave that nightmare buried in dark northern wood. Even now I awaken gripped in terror remembering the shrieks, the smells, and soulless red eyes glowing out of the abyss within blackened trees – the Wendigos' haunted forest domain. However hard I try, I cannot shake the dread that someday those gnarled claws and rancid breath will find me again across the years. For though physically I escaped the Wendigos' grasp, my dreams will belong to those ravenous demons forevermore.

# STORY 4

When I was ten, my mom met a man online named Stan who lived in a secluded cabin deep in the Minnesota wilderness. After a year, we packed up from Illinois and went to live with Stan. Though nervous at first, my siblings and I grew to love the tranquil woods surrounding his remote home. Stan taught us skills for thriving in the harsh environment, from outdoor survival to defending against vicious predators that roamed the endless dark forests. Little did we know true horror lurked right outside our door.

Stan delighted in telling campfire tales, but none gripped us kids like his stories of the Wendigo. According to ancient Ojibwe legends, this ghoulish beast once haunted these very forests, a skeletal specter over 15 feet tall with glowing eyes, yellow fangs, and a hunger for human flesh that was never satisfied. He claimed to have seen the demonic creature stalking the woods at night. We dismissed his stories...at first.

One summer night while Stan and Mom were away, my siblings and I played games outside until dusk. As darkness crept through the imposing spruces, I was overwhelmed by a sudden, inexplicable terror. My sister began crying that she felt unseen eyes watching us. We soon realized we all sensed the same lurking dread. Fleeing in panic through the darkened forest, we heard vicious snarls and the trees shaking violently around us as if huge claws raked their bark.

Bursting from the tree line, the cabin offered little respite - I glimpsed an emaciated ghoul peering through the windows! Glowing red eyes sunken in yellowed flesh pulled tight across its skeletal face. It smashed the glass and squeezed inside, horns scraping the ceiling. We cowered screaming as its raspy voice gurgled our names, tongue dripping with saliva. A crash from the kitchen hinted that more lurked outside.

These were no mere beasts but demons of Ojibwe legend stalking us through the shadows! We realized in horror that Stan's terrifying tales had come alive - the insatiable Wendigos had returned to claim our flesh and souls!

Just then headlights appeared down the drive. The creature shrieked in rage and vanished into the night, along with its prowling companions. Mom found us sobbing wrecks. Despite Stan's warnings, she refused to accept his tales were real...until she saw the smashed windows and deer-like tracks crossing the mudroom floor.

We armed ourselves with guns and knives, jumping at every creak and thump thereafter. The protective seal between reality and nightmare legends had been shattered, letting loose these lanky horrors from the forest's heart. Their glowing eyes still haunt my dreams, peering from the darkness, waiting to finish their gruesome feast.

# STORY 5

I'll never forget that fateful camping trip when I was nine years old and the forests of northern Wisconsin became a terrifying hunting ground. Those endless dark woods were my treasured escape until I gazed into hellish red eyes and discovered their ancient protector...the starving, flesh-craving Wendigo.

My friends and I were typical kids back then,

spending long summer days swimming, playing games, and exploring the dense pine barrens surrounding our remote camp. I had grown up in Wisconsin and was no stranger to the wilderness, often disappearing on solo hikes for hours without a care. But once night fell, so too did an oppressive dread. I couldn't shake rumors of a beast in local Ojibwe tales, the ominous Wendigo, said to stalk these same woods for eternal centuries.

According to whispered legends around dying fires, the towering and skeletal Wendigo was a demonic spirit able to enter and transform men into cold-hearted cannibals. Its glowing eyes pierced the darkest thickets in search of victims, sweeping victims into its terrible embrace with impossible speed on clawed feet or forcing their surrender with deafening cries and shrieks that carried for miles. Many vanished without a trace, as if the bottomless Northwoods simply swallowed them whole to feed the immortal creature's endless greed. We teased and spooked each other with these stories, but I always suspected a kernel of truth hid within the folklore...as if uttering its name too loudly might summon the flesh-starved monster into our reality.

It was dusk when I set off alone down the trail toward our favorite swimming hole, intent on cooling off as daylight faded. I was lost in thought about Wendigo tales when an unsettling awareness that something tracked my movement in the brush made my heart skip.

Scanning the thick forest lining the path, I discovered a hulking form atop a nearby boulder...and wished with all my being that I hadn't.

My mind reeled in disbelief. It crouched upright like a withered corpse, skeletal frame draped in pallid flesh that looked ready to slough off completely. I guessed it to stand at least 15 feet tall. Curving horns grew from its bald head above familiar vibrant red eyes that shone with predatory focus. As it peered down at me, the wraith flashed a grin across its wolfish muzzle, revealing rows of jagged yellow fangs.

Every nerve ignited with visceral revolt and my legs trembled, rooted in place by shock and primal horror. This was no man nor ordinary animal, but the demonic fiend of regional infamy...the insatiable Wendigo indeed did exist! My panicked mind raced as I accepted my gruesome death, already hearing the attended screams of past victims echoing in the monster's unearthly cries. As if reading my thoughts, the towering creature threw back its head, unleashing a blistering shriek that struck like lightning and burst through the woods.

The impossible sound jolted life back into my limbs. Heart throbbing in my ears, I fled that cursed forest, stumbling in mad panic as the monster's screeches gave chase. Bursting into camp moments later soaked in tears, my father's typical dismissal of "overactive imagination" only enraged me further. But I knew what I had witnessed - the emaciated specter wandering ancient Ojibwe tales for centuries had awakened to feed once more.

Safely back in Illinois days later, part of me wished I'd never returned from those Wisconsin woods. I jumped at branches scraping my window for weeks after, still hearing shrieks splitting the night air. As the years passed without further sign, I managed to convince myself it was all a twisted fantasy, a boogeyman explained away by logic and the mundane. But the spark of belief remains, keeping me alert for glowing eyes peering from the darkness. For somewhere deep in the Northwoods labyrinth, the ageless Wendigo skulks alone, wailing a tormented dirge...still desperately hungry.

# STORY 6

Nestled off Canada's eastern coasts, tranquil Prince Edward Island has always felt worlds removed from modernity. The island embodies eternal youth to me, a beloved summer escape where splendid beaches, colorful villages, and lush countryside forests compose an idyllic storybook paradise. But on one fateful camping trip deep in PEI's primordial woods as a boy, those childhood myths disintegrated. I gazed into endless abyssal eyes and witnessed the materializing of an ancient evil that haunts the island still...the gnawing horror called Wendigo.

Each summer my family faithfully returned to Prince Edward Island's elegant landscapes and sophisticated fishing resorts perched around meticulously groomed parks. But by age twelve I hungered to explore beyond the island's polished postcards and pristine holiday havens. Lured by wilderness intrinsically tied to my identity, I longed to forge deeper connections with the island's mysterious soul lurking within forgotten valleys and tangled forests brooding at PEI's uninhabited heart. Fool that I was, how little I truly understood what time-less secrets slumbered there.

After much pleading that summer, my father finally caved to my romantic notions of venturing off-trail into PEI's secluded backwoods to camp and fish for several days. Mercifully ignorant, we cheerily planned outings far removed from the island's bustling tourism industry, aiming to bond more profoundly with the landscape away from roads and marked camping grounds. Just the two of us embracing wild forests like so many Mi'kmaq tribes had centuries before modernity conquered their beloved hunting territories. Were we already trespassing into cursed lands better left undisturbed?

We departed on a glorious June morning beaming

with enthusiasm, oblivious to the darkness awaiting us in that primeval place sequestered from humanity and progress. Hours of breathless anticipation climaxed as glorious views announced our arrival into a sprawling valley cradled by densely wild hills. An ancient river threaded the valley's lush floor, reflecting the vibrant green forests hemming us in on all sides. Having brought only enough supplies for four days of isolated camping, I was intoxicated by the valley's paradisiacal perfection...never comprehending it already sheltered terrors from beyond time hunting there.

By midday we had pitched a cozy campsite on the lazily flowing river's mossy banks then eagerly cast our fishing lines again and again as afternoon dissolved toward dusk. Absorbed in our activities amidst a spectacular landscape apparently untouched for centuries, an ominous unease slowly registered only peripherally. As I reeled in yet another prize catch, the pungent aroma of death invaded my senses. Recoiling instinctively, I wondered if some small creature was decomposing nearby as Dad too suddenly stiffened, wrinkling his nose in revulsion. Then he murmured apologetically about the stench likely being related to restocking the river with extra fish earlier that season. I nodded uneasily before failing to hook a large and rather forceful fish tugging against my line. Preoccupied, I again dismissed the malodor as unusual but innocuous forest scents carried by still air. If only I had recognized Death's signature perfume when it caressed us, perhaps things could have ended differently.

My father had just retrieved a roaring fire from our campsite to cook dinner when the attack struck without warning. An earsplitting shriek exploded from the forest, splitting the dusk like a thunderclap and seeming to shake reality itself. Birds erupted in clouds from trembling branches while Dad and I crumpled to our knees, rural folks instinctually recognizing the piercing hunting cry of something that kills mercilessly. Rotten odors assaulted me once more and suddenly congealed into hideous meaning. Something impossibly massive yet emanating grave hunger was barreling toward us with lightning speed from the gloomy forest recesses concealing the valley's perimeter.

My heart convulsed as adrenaline flooded through me. Too terrified to scream, I somehow stumbled upright while Dad regained his own footing. Together we turned to confront whatever had found us in that forgotten place so far from inhabited shores. Fate itself recoiled as the devil emerged.

Materializing from tendrils of fog appeared an apparition seeming dredged from the abyssal depths of nightmare; I beheld the ageless phantom itself named Wendigo. My mind shuddered attempting to comprehend the urgently retreating figure before me. Impossibly gaunt body parts jutted at severe angles from its towering frame slinking almost double over. I realized this crooked posture was from the creature possessing a height nearing 15 feet...supported upon almost fleshless limbs! Indeed its entire body appeared wrapped in an ashen cowl of some tissue so grey and taunt that every bone protruded grotesquely. Like a cadaver granted hellish animation by forces opposed to nature itself, the fiend's lidless eyes smoldered a spectral crimson glare beneath a naked scalp cresting its elongated face. Fangs yellow as amber and curved to rend oblivion crowned its horned skull helm for conquering Death himself rose from brow to crown. Every atom radiated insatiable hunger and ancient contempt.

This was no earthly animal but supernatural terror spawned from regional folklores and nightmares. Each detail and nuance of the fiend reflected icons immortalized for centuries by Canada's First Nations...the mythic and accursed Wendigo itself stalked before me!

My mind ruptured attempting to process that lethal enormity grinning in anticipation mere yards away. I wanted to wail apologies for trespassing upon its cursed hunting grounds but astonishment choked such notions. There could be no negotiating for life or mercy with this sinister assembly of prehistoric bones and desires. It had lurked here consuming unwary humans since before men kept records. We were only meat...and it was so very, very famished.

A keening noise escaped my throat. As if interpreting that utterance as hopeless resignation, the towering Wendigo reared upright almost sluggishly with arms grotesquely elongated and twig-like fingers adorned by jagged claws curled eagerly. Another roar unlike any natural animal cry burst from behind its jutting fangs. Still I stood paralyzed in mortal dread, watching hypnotically as the fiend braced gnarled legs...then charged us faster than I would have believed possible.

I heard my father shouting to run even as we both stumbled backwards in tandem. The pursuing Hellbeast rapidly closed the gap with vehement shrieks as I blindly turned to flee downriver. Glancing over my shoulder long enough to glimpse my dad recklessly hurl a large rock he had scooped up towards the monster's torso in desperation, earning an enraged howl. Already I imagined feeling jagged claws rend both spine and flesh as the Wendigo seized me for its gruesome feast...

I plunged heedlessly into the blood-frigid river upon which we had floated our tiny boat earlier while indulging such carefree dreams. Staggering waist-deep into the racing current, I prayed the biting cold might slow our stalker or even allow escape if we could launch the canoe. But suddenly the empty little craft swept past as the current had broken it from shore. Now truly defenseless, I whirled expecting to see red eyes boring into mine at last. To my astonished relief, no towering demon-like shape darkened the dusk but surely it lurked near. Heaving frantically while searching for Dad, I spotted him crawling onto shore clutching the camp stove as sole weapon against the unseen menace undoubtedly poised to finish us off beyond sight.

Then fragmented memories of region myths invaded my bewildered mind...stories of ancient curses and pacts with night spirits. Terrified tribal shamans attempting to combat this self-same creature we now faced, intoning forbidden incantations calling flames from their very spirits to repel...and at best merely evade the unholy monstrosity named Wendigo! Cowering in muddy reeds as I listened desperately for sounds of the lurking Devil, revelation suddenly burned bright - fire had threatened all legendary Wendigos since First Nations oral records began. Was flames our single pathetic chance for salvation?

I must have dredged pine branches aiming to somehow spark them alight as the faint steady roar of Dad's camp stove igniting echoed through the thickening gloom. Then that dreaded piercing cry split the trees again denting my resolve. Somehow I stumbled onto shore mere feet from my deathly pale father now wielding the makeshift torch against leathery sinew rushing us from the darkness once more. Raising my own smoldering brand, I saw malevolent eyes reflecting the flames as our would-be killer recoiled with a roar. The smell of our campfire now seemed to disorient the Wendigo as we retreated unevenly downriver clinging to the precious flames keeping gnashing fangs and talons at bay...for the present.

No words were shared upon finally regaining the beach and collapsing into Dad's truck after hours of staggering slowly through the fading night, flinching at every forest sound while exhaustion and stress nearly killed us as surely as the resurrected myths stalking implacably just behind the blazing brands. Returned to humanity as the eastern seaboard sky beckoned dawn, I dared not speak of what had transpired in those fatefully beautiful valley woods now a haunted graveyard harboring a guardian seemingly spawned from Canada's historic nightmares. I only knew blissful Prince Edward Island's elegance would never again conceal its menacing chaos churning eternally in the primordial darkness...and the insatiable immortal monster named Wendigo still creeps somewhere in those lonely pines.

## STORY 7

My family's move from Wyoming to rural Maine was a culture shock, trading endless prairies for dark ancient forests surrounding our secluded home. I was nine when we left behind friends for this reclusive life in New England's shadowy woods. My brother and I embraced adventure outdoors, naively trespassing into the hunting grounds of a legendary horror that hungered insatiably for human flesh...the accursed Wendigo.

By day, the forest's tranquility concealed the madness lurking within its endless spruce and fog-veiled clearings. But at night, my imagination conjured the ghastly screams echoing outside my window...as if lost souls cried warnings from beyond the void. Local tribes once whispered of wicked spirits named Wendigo that stalked these woods, possessing men's minds and bringing agony to victims in the icy darkness. When desolate winter shrouded the remote homestead even darker, I further dreaded facing the unknown outside our walls.

Restless one morning, my brother and I set off to explore beyond the unseen property borders. The surrounding woods appeared pristine, yet we couldn't escape the certainty of lurking eyes tracking us. No birds filled the silence with their songs. We discovered a rushing creek and conspired to return with fishing poles, delighted to claim the spot as our secret sanctuary from loneliness. Parting ways, my brother hurried home through the still woods while I perched listening to the water, unnerved by the absence of animals. Then the foliage usually masking the forest floor shuddered slightly across the stream. Where nothing lived before, now hulked a form hunkered down watching the water intently.

I sat hypnotized by the creature's impossible height and unnatural proportions. Shaggy fur draped its hulking shoulders above impossibly gangly arms curled before its crouched body. Fearing a bear, I froze in place as the misshapen head cleaved through the creek's surface. I stifled a gasp when it withdrew clutching a large fish in its mouth lined by rows of jagged yellow teeth. Relief washed over me realizing no bear or mundane animal crouched yards away, but confusion quickly replaced it. If not nature's beast, then what entity had I disturbed?

As it shifted, dread crept from the darkest recess of my soul. The creature rose upright upon gangly legs doubled-jointed like a fiend from hell. Standing fully erect well over 12 feet, its emaciated body appeared wrapped in leathered flesh streaked grey and yellow pulled taut across protruding rib bones. Lank arms dangled passed its knees ending in gnarled talons built to shred prey. Slowly it turned to face me, frozen in terror. Familiar tribal folklore became flesh. Within that bloodless face sunken eyes smoldered malevolence across the centuries...the insatiable glowing orbs of the man-eating phantom named Wendigo!

I managed a muted whimper while scrambling backward. Anger contorted the fiend's lips, revealing rows of jagged crooked fangs capable of crushing bone. My mind recoiled knowing those gnarled talons hungered to disembowel me. Then a resounding crackle pierced the silence - my brother's panicked voice blaring urgently through the walkie-talkie. The monster's head snapped toward the shattering noise, locking its predatory glare upon my helpless form. It unleashed an ungodly roar that transmuted blood to ice. I turned and fled blindly through whipping branches as sanity unraveled.

That bellowing cry of outrage and crimson eyes aflame with preternatural intelligence burned indelibly into memory while I crashed wildly through the haunted forest. The stench of fungal decay cloyed in my nostrils promising perils worse than death. Somehow I burst from those accursed woods into our yard and fell wailing before my disbelieving family. Though I sensed the brooding trees concealing grisly secrets, ma and pa insisted imagination had warped some wild animal into a boogeyman like from regional folk tales. But subsequent frozen nights, I lay awake tracking unholy screams echoing through the abyssal forest...knowing the man-eating terror named Wendigo yet haunted the ancient pines craving my tender flesh.

We dared not speak what we all feared when neighboring homesteads sat abruptly abandoned before that bitter winter's end. Wendigo fangs surely claimed those lost souls. When spring finally thawed the blanketed wilderness, revealing no trace of the missing, we packed swiftly for Louisiana without a backwards glance. But the Wendigo is eternal, its bloodlust never sated. I pray those glowing eyes never mark me again in the few nights my dreams stray beyond society into untamed forests...where starlit shadows disguise the lurking hollow-eyed demon waiting patiently to finish its feast.

# PUBLISHER'S EXCERPT 1

## FROM ABOVE: UFO ENCOUNTERS: VOLUME 1

## ENCOUNTER 1

My encounter happened when I was just a little boy in the nineteen sixties in Pennsylvania. I lived in the middle of nowhere and I've recently come to find that what I witnessed one spring night is something that isn't unique to me or the area I lived in at the time. There are people all over the country who have reported seeing very similar things in areas that are all similar as far as their geography. Mainly, it happened every single time to someone who was, for one reason or another, in some deep woods or the middle of a forest. I was an only child at the time and one of the things my parents and I would love to do together would be to spend time out in nature. We were one of the only families in a three block radius that had our own pool in the backyard and it made my house a popular spot for the kids in the area. My parents didn't mind and loved having not only the kids there but their parents as well. As for me, I was an outcast and didn't really fit in with the other kids my age. As I got older I realized it's just because I was a little more mature and into things like reading and writing as opposed to playing games and purposely hurting myself like the other little boys I knew. Kids will be kids and I was picked on a lot. I never told my parents about it though because I was embarrassed but mainly it was because the kids who were bullying me relentlessly were some of the same ones who would be at my house with their parents, pretending to be my friend every day during the summer months when the pool was open. I only mention all of that because it has to do with why I was in the woods in the first place, after dark, when I was only seven years old.

It was a typical summer afternoon and the backyard was filled with kids and our parents sat on the deck while my dad grilled and they all listened to music. We would play the usual kid games and while most of the boys there were my tormentors at any other time of year, the girls and a few boys who were exceptions to that rule were also there. There were approximately twelve of us in total and we were actually having a good time. Eventually it was time to eat dinner and we all got out of the pool and sat at the table designated for the children. We laughed and joked until it was time for everyone to go home. By the time nine o'clock rolled around everyone was gone and my mother wanted me to get ready for bed. I did as I was told and after she tucked me in I went right to sleep. It was around midnight when I heard tapping at my first floor window. I jumped up and at first I was scared but when I looked it was some of the older kids from the neighborhood. Two of them, to be exact, and they wanted to know if I wanted to go with them to help the one boy find his lost puppy. They were around eleven years old and the older brothers of some of the kids who had been there at the pool party that day. They were there too so I knew and somewhat trusted them. It didn't occur to my seven year old mind that there was no reason for kids to be knocking on my window and asking me to sneak out when if someone really needed help their parents would have gone to the front door and rang the doorbell or called on the phone. I was eager to help and eager to please and so I quickly agreed to help them.

I got out of bed and put my sneakers on. I went to the back door and silently snuck out of my house. I know it seems like I was a little young but if you think back on being that age you might find that you would have also done anything, including things that were far out of your character, to impress the older kids. If not, then understand that's what was in it for me, or so I hoped and thought. I thought if I could be the one to find the lost kitten then the other kids would be my friend or at the very least they would leave me alone and stop constantly bullying me. I had no idea I was walking into a trap. I went outside and entered the backyard where the two older boys waited for me. We were whispering and they told me that they saw the kitten leave out the back door of the house when it was accidentally left open and that it had run into the woods. I was terrified of those woods at night and even when me and some of the other kids would play in them, it was never at nighttime and I was even scared of being in them during the day. However, a lot was at stake for me and I tried my best to be brave and help them. They seemed really sad and so I asked them how I could help. They told me to go into the woods with them and that we would all split up. Then they handed me a flashlight and told me to follow them. I did as I was told and before I knew it I was a fifteen minute walk into the middle of the woods and all by myself. I was looking for the kitten and trying to lure it out of wherever it could have been hiding. I was scared but trying not to think about it. I lived in a good neighborhood, I reasoned, and monsters weren't real anyway.

After I had been out there for a half hour though it dawned on me that the other two kids should have met me by then and I was getting nervous that they had somehow tricked me. I was also concerned that we were all going to get into trouble because it crossed my mind that perhaps they hadn't met me yet because they were lost too. I was definitely lost and I knew that because I hadn't been paying much attention to where I was going because I thought that the other two kids were close by and they had promised to lead me back home if we hadn't found the kitten within a half hour of searching. I looked at my watch and it had been longer than that and I started to tremble and cry. I was wailing and just as I started to hyperventilate, the other two boys came out of some nearby trees, pointing and laughing at me, calling me all kinds of names. Before I even had a chance to react to that though we all heard a sound that almost knocked us off our feet. We all had to cover our ears because the shrieking sound was so invasive, our noses actually all started to bleed at the same time. We kept our heads down and with our hands on our ears tried to yell to one another, asking what in the world that noise was. I was convinced they had done something to further my humiliation and that the incredibly annoying and grating shrieking sound had been just another part of it. They were crying too though and once I noticed that I knew we were all in big trouble. There was a giant flash of light in the sky and suddenly the noise stopped. The three of us were just standing there, somewhat huddled together when we realized that not only could we not hear the shrieking sound anymore but we couldn't hear anything at all. It wasn't only that the whole forest had gone silent but it was more than that. It seemed like the whole world had gone silent and as we stood there, we watched in silence as a gigantic disc that was glowing red lowered from the sky, right from where the flash had been, and hovered a few feet above the ground. It was about two yards away from us at that time. I saw the kids that I was with and their lips were moving but I couldn't hear them for some reason and I started to panic, thinking the noise had somehow made me go deaf permanently. I asked them what they were saying but they didn't seem to hear me and in fact, I didn't hear myself in my own ears either which further perpetuated the terror I was already experiencing.

The next thing I know they took off running back towards what I figured was the direction of their house.

They knew where they were going after all, unlike myself who was terrified and lost in the darkness of the forest in the middle of the night at only seven years old and faced with some unknown disc that had come down from the sky. It sounded like something was happening to me that I had only known could happen in some of the comic books I snuck around reading all the time. Suddenly there was a loud noise, one that I actually heard, but the ground also shook from it somewhat. I was already unsteady on my feet and fell to the ground. It sounded like metal scraping against metal and I saw that some sort of door had opened up on the disc and something was coming out of it. I stood up quickly and realized that I could hear again, even though the forest had gone quiet. Hearing nothing but silence and not being able to hear are two completely different things. There was another flash and loud bang and then two giant beings were standing there in front of me, just staring at me. I could only stare back as I urinated in my pajamas. They were nine feet tall, at least, and they looked like an average robot. By that I mean that they were similar to Alice, the robot maid in the cartoon series The Jetsons. I knew that because it had become one of my favorite cartoons to watch on a Saturday morning. They weren't gray or silver though but red. They had the pointy antennas on top of their robot heads and they were silent.

They looked me up and down several times and each time they would turn and look at one another immediately after. I realize now that they were more than likely engaged in some sort of telepathic communication with one another. I could not hear what they were saying though and it looked like they weren't saying anything at all. They then proceeded to pull something out of one of the little doors in their bodies, somewhere around where humans put pockets in the front of their jeans. I guess the little doors on those robots functioned the same way. I thought for sure it was going to be a laser beam that would disintegrate me entirely upon contact but it looked like little beakers with lids and they looked empty. The robots stuck the little beakers in the dirt, scooped some up and into it and then put the lid on. They then put the beakers, or whatever they were, full of dirt right back into their "pockets" and turned to look at me one more time. They then turned in unison and walked the same way back to the ship. There was a quick flash of red before it zoomed off into the night sky and was gone before I finished blinking. I was so confused, startled, terrified, and awestruck I didn't know what to do. Before I knew it I heard my dad's concerned voice screaming through the woods for me. I yelled back and immediately started crying hysterically until he found me and carried me home. He helped me clean myself up and put me back in bed where I slept the entire night and the whole next day. I had to tell my parents what happened and I told them everything. The problem is they didn't know which part to believe and to their credit they believed me wholeheartedly about the two boys luring me into the woods in the first place. My mother immediately called their mother and an hour later they were at my house apologizing. They didn't mention the spaceship and neither did I, at least not on front of them. I thought my parents would ask them, if for no other reason than to confirm my story but they didn't. In fact, they never mentioned it again until years later.

My father eventually asked me, when I was in my twenties, what had really happened that night. I told him and he said that he never saw anything and he had been out there looking for me for hours. That was weird because I thought I was only out there for an hour and a half at most. Turns out it had been three hours and my dad had been minutes away from giving up and going back to the house to call the police. He believed me though, after I told him once I was older and he actually apologized to me for not taking me more seriously when I told him the first time, when I was seven. I figured I forgave him already because what would he and my mother really have been able to do with that information should they have believed me anyway? I never saw anything like that again but nowadays I know more than ever that I saw some sort of extraterrestrials and their craft. I figured with all of the alleged disclosures being made, I could write about my story now without fear of too much ridicule. Thanks

―――――

## FROM ABOVE: UFO ENCOUNTERS

## STORY 8

I still wake up screaming some nights even though it's been years since I first came across that.... That thing out in the woods. It was the middle of December and snowing but that had nothing to do with what happened to us, despite what some skeptics would like to believe. They blame it on hypothermia and whatever else they can think of so that they don't have to face the reality of what we saw and the implications for humanity if they were to believe it was real. I know that I saw and felt out there and no one will ever convince me otherwise. It had evil in its eyes older than even the ancient trees that fill that particular forest, and it wanted me as its next meal so it could hibernate and fend off the winter storms. My girlfriend Stacey and I were driving out from the city so that we could spend Christmas with my uncle Jerry. He lives on a little crop farm, far out from where the rural highway ends and in a very isolated area. He's very isolated, even for someone who lives all alone with no neighbors and with nothing but the dense and desolate forest surrounding him to keep him company. Stacy was asleep in the passenger seat and I drove, following Jerry's scribbled directions down winding dirt roads flanked by bare trees and with hard snow and frost crunching underneath my tires. The sky was already fading to indigo when my phone lost signal, so I figured we must be getting really close to the turn off for the long, winding road that led to the even longer driveway. I had somewhat stopped paying close enough attention once the last farm lights disappeared from view and I got us turned around. I suddenly realized that we were driving down the wrong snowy trail that starts leading straight into the forest itself after a few miles, just as night fully fell to make the shadows of the trees look deeper than they already were.

Now, I had grown up in a nearby town to where my uncle lived and I spent a ton of time at his house when I was little and all throughout the time I was growing up. Jerry's house was where we would all gather as a family, dozens of us, and celebrate or whatever it was we were getting together for at any given time and he and many other members of my family had always warned me to steer clear of roaming too close to that ancient forest, especially come late fall and winter. They said evil spirits lurked within that the Native Indians long ago called "lycanthropes." I always scoffed at the legends, and of my family's deep belief in them, as did most of the kids in the family. While we laughed though, most of the adults in town- not just my family- would put up warding totems at the forest's edge to keep what they called "the bad medicine" out and off of their properties and their land. Most of them lived pressed up against the forest, all over the town. I really started to get annoyed with the constant superstitions in my family, particularly surrounding the wendigo, when I moved to the nearest big city and I would go back and visit. It's like nothing ever changed and it was something they talked about and warned those of us from the younger generations away from. I just figured their boogeyman was a silly tall tale meant to spook kids. I was too cocky by not taking those old legends seriously, especially on the night I am telling you about now.  By the time I realized the dirt trail had gone from rutted to nearly overgrown, and we seemed to be winding aimlessly through pines and hemlocks so densely packed they blocked the rising moon, Stacey was awake and fussing about how I got us lost. Stacey and I hadn't been dating very long at the time and I was bringing her to meet my family for the first time. I was aching to impress her but seemingly, by the way she was acting about being lost, I was off to a lousy start. She immediately freaked out about her phone not having any signal and was getting more and more agitated as I tried my best to reassure her and calm her down. The truth was that while I was doing everything I could to ease her mind, I had no idea where I was or where to go next, to get us closer to my uncle's house.

I did my best to sound confident but out of nowhere the old legends I had grown up with about the wendigo started playing through my head and it became almost all that I could think of. I tried to find a good spot to turn around without it being too dangerous or risking us being stuck in a ditch and then stranded out in the middle of nowhere, but not too long after the third or fourth gulch we bounced through, I knew we were in trouble. The way the branches seemed to knot together was more twisted and claw-like, almost like they were reaching for my truck, put me more on edge. All the winding roots pushing up through the snowy dirt trail looked like bony fingers grasping to snag our tires too. It got so quiet in the forest around us, and it was only my truck's headlights cutting through the dark and lighting up sickly birches and needly pines. The sky was completely devoid of stars and there was no moon that night. I was driving really slowly at that point and something else struck me as very strange. There were no critters skittering around, dodging the tires, or generally running up and down the trees and across clearings to either side of us. It was like even nature knew better than to make a peep in that accursed place. The heavy silence seemed to weigh on us just as much as the darkness was. My chest started to feel tight and achy. Stacey kept praying under her breath next to me, while I felt myself starting to sweat big pools under my cap despite the vents blasting cold air from struggling against the steep gullies. Though I was raised to be somewhat religious, Stacey's prayers provided me with no comfort. I just felt like there was something evil out there with us and I was grateful we at least had the protection of the truck itself and that we weren't completely exposed out there. I couldn't see much and I was having a hard time finding my way through the forest, despite doing my best to stick to the wider trails and semi-roads that had been made from so many quads and other off-road vehicles throughout who knew how many years. I wanted to scream at Stacey to shut up and the thought itself startled me as I wasn't the kind of guy who yelled at a woman for doing something as simple as praying next to me for my own safety as well as hers, but I was just about to yell at her to shut the hell up when something happened. I spotted something on the left side that made me slam the brakes and dangerously attempt to whip the truck around if the trail was wide enough.

There at the edge of my high beam's reach were three tall nasty-looking log totems standing in a winter-dead bramble patch, with these little bowls near the tops that I bet once held fire. They were carved with twisting shapes and faces that looked pained, like lost souls had somehow been captured in the wood. Drawings of bones and frightful animals covered the poles too, and the tallest had a huge antlered skull atop it. All of the creeping vines and thorns pulling the totems slightly askew made my breath catch sharply, and empty black eye sockets seemed to follow me as we crept past them slowly. These weren't decorations either. I sensed that they were warnings from whoever had been living out here before the forest swallowed everything up. I suddenly remembered my grandmother always yelling about keeping wicked things chained outside and I didn't know why that popped into my head right then but it made me so scared I almost couldn't think straight anymore. I tried to pull myself together. I had already decided that Stacey wasn't the girl for me, just based off of her attitude about my making a mistake and accidentally getting us lost, plus how cold she was being to me just then as I profusely apologized to her about it, but I also didn't want to seem like I was scared either. Stacey suddenly looked at me and told me that we shouldn't be there because we hadn't been invited and we didn't have a blessing. I was white knuckling the wheel when I felt Stacey's hand grab my left shoulder fiercely, jolting me back from leaning toward the totems still staring behind us like they were starving and we were the answer. Her long red nails dug in as she screeched directly into my ear to stop quickly. My foot slammed on the brake without thinking, mainly from surprise, and also because of the weird thing she had just said right before she so violently grabbed me. I felt the truck fishtail on the icy trail a bit before I eased us to a halt as carefully as I could. Stacey was panting hard and clinging to me, so I tried calming her with an apology. Only when I glanced in her direction finally, did I see her horrified gaze was locked on something outside of the window instead.

Afraid to follow her eyes, I turned slowly, my muscles seizing up to follow her stare down the narrow beam of my headlights. There at the far edge just inside the tree line hunkered the biggest wolf I'd ever seen, and I had been camping my whole life with my dad and my whole family when I was growing up. It didn't take much more than a glance to realize that it wasn't an ordinary wolf. It stood easily on its hind legs just like any human being would stand and its front paws dangled out in front of it like some sort of freakish outstretched arms. From where we were it was also easy to tell that the monstrous creature was nearly as tall as an average horse. Its mangy gray fur barely covered what looked like loose sick flesh sagging off a starved frame with ribs poking everywhere. It was disgusting and looked sickly. Despite it hunkering down like it was injured, I got the sense that it could still move and lunge as quickly as a viper. When our lights brushed over its face, I saw bloody flesh stretched tight over a snout of jagged fangs that were longer than a small hunting knife and its cloudy yellow eyes pierced out of its bony skull. It was staring right back at me, with those hideous and terrifying eyes shining with cunning and evil. The worst part was that I could've sworn that the beast was grinning widely, murderously, back at me. Stacey's nails biting my shoulder was finally what snapped me from staring frozen at the crooked creature. I fumbled throwing my rig in reverse as she started shrieking like a maniac, and though I didn't blame her as I was barely keeping myself from doing the same, she was making the cabin echo and pound in my head. No way that wolf hadn't heard her carrying on with its pointy ears twitching toward our truck as I tried backing up quickly and daring down the narrow and rutted trail. As soon as I tried turning us back the way we came, the "wolf" let out a soul-curdling howl that sounded like it was half human and the other half was nothing but pain and fury. The ghastly crying noise of it made my teeth chatter as we swerved away quickly. Just when I thought it couldn't get more surreal or terrifying, not to mention dangerous, it started chasing us on all fours like a bat out of hell.

I stomped the gas hard as we rocketed blindly through naked black branches and buried rocks, praying we'd find the trail we were initially supposed to be on, before I had gotten us so desperately lost. Stacey must've been in shock because she took to screaming every time tree limbs scratched against the doors- which was the whole time. Twisting around a tight bend, I swore I glimpsed those yellow predator eyes cutting through my rear windshield. It looked hungry, but worse than that, it had been able to keep up with my truck despite my going at least forty miles per hour, maybe more. On top of everything else that was wrong with that animal and with the situation itself, it dawned on me what I knew all along. Wolves aren't supposed to hunt people alone. However, this foul beast seemed to just want to catch us and finish us off. I felt the truck fishtailing again as I haphazardly glanced back to see if it was still chasing us, catching flickers of sagging fur and snapping fangs always at our bumper somehow. A turn or two later, Stacey was begging me to stop so she could run, or shoot it, or anything other than to have to be in the truck, being chased by some strange and seemingly demonic creature wearing a wolf suit, as we tore through woods so dark and icy we were guaranteed to crash and basically hand ourselves over to it when we did so. There was no way we would survive if we crashed, even if we survived the initial crash, because that thing was looking to eat us and we both knew that surer than we knew anything else in this life at that time. She screamed at me about my "damn cursed driving"- her words, not mind. But to be fair, it was a fair assessment. She just didn't seem to be considering that I was just as terrified and confused as she was. Honestly, she didn't seem to care and a part of me wanted to stop the car and let her get out and take her chances running. She was that obnoxious. But I suppressed that urge and tried to maintain a better focus on my driving and whatever was ahead and in front of us. Honestly, screeching to a stop and letting her flee seemed our best hope if it slowed that monster from ripping into my skull to get my brain as we spun out wrecked. I know what you must be thinking, but please reserve your judgment until you're in the same situation and come out of it without thinking the same things as I was. For your sake though I pray you never are.

Just as I geared myself to hit the brakes as soon as the ground leveled some, I spotted a faint warm light maybe fifty yards ahead filtering through skeletal tree trunks and slammed my palm down on my busted horn for as long as I could. An old hunter's shack with half its tin roof caved in and porch beams rotting sat tucked thirty feet off our makeshift trail, glowing from a lantern left on inside. As we careened closer, I saw the sagging homestead also had protective totems circling it identically carved as the ones we passed earlier that night. My headlights flashed over a buck skull and charred bones scattered before those crooked hand-hewn poles as I spun us sideways, skidding to a stop parked across the trail facing back toward the oncoming predator for a final stand. The second our tires quit screeching, Stacey was out of her door and racing toward that dismal hut, leaving me dizzy from adrenaline and fear. Her fiery hair streamed behind as she bounded recklessly for those wards meant to guard off wicked spirits. Part of me wanted to yell that she was crazy, trusting such superstitious totems but, the thing was, glancing down the trail where my lights illuminated those carved warnings, I somehow knew their twisted faces were all too real. I knew it in my bones because of what I had been taught growing up. What stalked us through this accursed forest wasn't any ordinary animal at all, but a lycanthrope- one of those werewolves that my relatives and their ancestors as well as everyone else in the area where I had grown up, where Stacey and I were just then, tried keeping buried outside where the cold could chain its cruel heart for eternity. I watched helplessly as Stacey crossed the circle of those wicked totems so old and weather-worn they were nearly fused with the buried bones of owners unknown. More than likely, from what I knew, they were from long dead animals and not from human beings at all. However, that depended on how old they were and the beliefs of the person who constructed them. Stacey stumbled up rotting planks to yank savagely on the shack's boarded door just as I heard branches crunching loud down the trail. She screamed for help and the door to the half fallen shack swung open. A man with a gun answered the door and looking past her and then past me, pulled her inside and screamed for me to follow them. I didn't hesitate and before long Stacey and I were inside and the old man was firing shots off into the woods where we had just come from. He turned and looked at us after locking the door with triple locks. I finally breathed a sigh of relief.

Luckily the old man was gentle and understood what we were telling him. He stayed up with us for hours, making sure the creature didn't get close to the door, which he said the totems outside would make sure of. He reiterated all of the old legends my family had always told me and I felt foolish forever mocking it at all. Stacey finally fell asleep and so did I, and in the morning the old man gave us directions to my uncle's house, which he knew well because that was the type of area he lived in. Everyone knew everyone else. I told him and the rest of my family what had happened to us and they all crossed themselves and said prayers over us and eventually it was time to go home. We refused to go outside at all at night, not that we had much reason to. We had a great time, except for the constant, underlying fear from our first night and the whole way home we made sure we weren't driving at night at all. We stayed in a motel for the one overnight. It would take to get home. Stacey and I didn't speak much once we got home and eventually we didn't speak at all. I know the story I just told you will seem unlikely and far-fetched to most people but like I already said, it's up to you what you want to believe. As for me, I know what I saw and I had two witnesses to it. My family believes me but the authorities never did. Not that I called them at the time but my uncle reported it afterwards and they called me to question me about it. It's over now and that was more than a decade ago. I have nightmares about it and can't hike, camp or hunt anymore and in fact I don't go into the woods at all. Not for any reason. Thanks for taking the time to read my story and for allowing me to tell it. I think it's important that the so-called "old legends" aren't lost to time or forgotten, and that the younger generations learn the importance of respecting them. And of respecting the traditions surrounding them. Staccy and I would have definitely been killed that night and I know that for certain because that creature had no intention of stopping its relentless and tireless pursuit of my vehicle and other than the sun suddenly rising early, which is impossible, we didn't stand a chance. I still talk to the guy who helped us out that night and will be eternally grateful to him for all he did for us.

# STORY 9

I know what I saw that day in those woods and I know it was real. It doesn't matter at all that the police acted like I was just another hiker that got turned around in the early winter chill and had maybe gone a little loopy from exhaustion. No one believed me back then, not even the people who knew me best or who were the closest to me but I never backed down. Reality is the truth and that's that, no matter who does or doesn't believe it. They weren't out there with me. It was just me wandering all alone under those towering oaks and birches that seemed to block out the very sun itself, leaving things as dim as if it had been closer to dusk than to midday. I went into the deep forest to clear my head, Just like I always had, throughout my whole life and ever since I was little, when things got bad and I was having a hard time at home or in school. See, the woods I was in were near an old park that had been there for at least a half a century at the time and I found a spot inside to hide away where I thought no one would ever be able to find me. It was my hideout as a kid where I'd play pretend about going on adventures, conjuring up dreams of exploring magical worlds where no one could bother me and where no one else was welcome. I always felt so safe there playing games and pretending fairies under the dark firs for hours, knowing their thick needles would keep me hidden if need be. Once I grew up and got married I felt like I had no choice but to give up those old trails and take care of my family. I never told my husband, Eddie, about that spot and honestly I don't think it ever came up. When I married Eddie he almost immediately got deployed and I moved closer to his parent's house in another city, somewhat far away from my childhood home, and my favorite childhood haunt. It's been a decade since we first moved to this town but a few weeks ago I got the brilliant idea to go and visit not only my parents for the first time this decade but also to go and visit my old childhood hiding spot.

It was a gloomy Autumn day but it wasn't raining and as I visited with my mom and dad, I just had this ache inside to go walk under those towering oaks and yellowing aspens like I did when I didn't have a care in the world and when life was much simpler- even if I didn't know that at the time. I got to the park trailhead early, just after dawn when a cool fog still clung to the forest floor, making each fern and low shrub look like they were covered in crystals. I was eager to get moving and warm myself up, so I didn't pay any attention to the heavy silence except for a murder of crows cawing angrily off in the distance. Those fire-orange and purple leaves sure were a beautiful and welcoming sight when I first entered the forest and started slowly walking along a trail I remembered and I was somewhat surprised I remembered it so well. I walked deeper and deeper into the woods. However, about two miles into my journey, when I got to the spot where the trail crossed a little creek, I started getting the weirdest sense of being watched from the dark thickets around me. There were no birds singing, I couldn't hear the crows cawing anymore and even the dumb squirrels and chipmunks seemed to hide from me as I picked up my pace. Even though the sky was bright blue above the autumn colors starting to blot out the sun, I suddenly felt a gloom settling on me that seemed to come from the shadows. Things were starting to feel really off, though I couldn't quite put my finger on what was making me feel that way. I also had the distinct feeling that something or someone was following me around and I had felt it from the moment I entered the park, like I was being watched, but the feeling grew much stronger when I reached the trails and got deeper into the woods. Regardless of how I was feeling, I kept trudging uphill, telling myself it was probably just a moose or somebody's big stray dog sniffing around behind me in the brush. But then I saw what looked like some kind of claw marks had dug deep into a huge maple, and there was sticky sap still oozing out of where the marks had been made. I tried to be reasonable and told myself that more than likely it had been from a bear, but I also reasoned that they seemed to be too high up for that. They definitely weren't climbing marks or anything like that. They were deep gouges and not normal or anything I had ever seen before and I got chills up and down my spine even though I was bundled up in the cold weather.

I could no longer ignore the nagging feeling inside that I wasn't alone out there and that it wasn't an animal that had been following me. I finally called out, asking the seemingly empty forest if anyone was out there. Of course, aside from a lone bird singing far away, there wasn't a response. There was still no sound at all. I started to call out again but thought better of it, thinking that perhaps I didn't want to alert who or whatever was out there to the fact that I was aware of them. Also, what if I was just being paranoid and my incessant yelling out to the air alerted some other threat or danger of not only my presence but my location as well. I noticed that the faraway bird was chirping the same four notes over and over again, almost incessantly and the lone sound added to the eeriness of the situation. I listened closer and suddenly it sounded like it wasn't a bird, but a small and childlike voice calling out and pleading for help. I thought I was losing my mind and told myself that it was just that I hadn't been there in so long or in the woods at all for any reason at all in the last decade, that perhaps the woods had lost their magic and wonder and weren't so much fun anymore. I tried to brush it off and I tried not to hear it but the call kept echoing through the trees for minutes on end, like it was warning me, till finally I turned off trail toward the ridge to get away from it. But I couldn't shake the nerves climbing up my back by then. When I got to a rocky clearing on the ridge that I knew gave a really nice view of the valley and all of all the patchwork of orange and yellow leaves below, I forced myself to shake it off. I told myself once again that I was getting all worked up over nothing and I decided to sit on a large boulder nearby to take a few deep breaths and calm myself a bit. I was determined to enjoy myself. This place meant too much to me and even if it wasn't as magical and wondrous as it had once been, I still desperately needed to feel like I belonged there. I can't explain it.

I sat there for about ten minutes surrounded by nothing but complete and totally unnatural silence. That's when I first heard heavy footsteps crunching through the underbrush fast and uneven, and it sounded like it was moving straight towards me from across the clearing. No twigs or leaves rustled though, and it was just heavy thudding of boots tromping closer through the tall grass. But the footfalls didn't walk normally. It was like one leg was lunging way ahead of the other with each stride, accompanied by this weird throaty kind of growl almost like a sick moose coughing up bile or something. With all the time I had spent in those woods, I knew the difference between an animal's steps and the footfalls of human beings and everything in between as well. I would have considered myself an expert on those types of sounds out there. I spun around looking for something huge to come barreling at me from the tree line, but the ridge was empty and quiet as a held breath. Scared as all hell now, I dashed towards a berry bramble and crouched down. I huddled there paralyzed for a long minute with my back turned from where I last heard it approaching, not even daring to peek behind me and trying not to breathe too heavily. The uneven feet just kept on stomping towards my hiding place, but I couldn't see anything human-sized over my shoulder yet. I actually couldn't see anything at all. I was just getting ready to jump out and run when I heard an inhuman scream pierce through the air. It was so loud it hurt my ears but it had no echo to it. It sounded somewhat like a cross between a wounded hawk shriek and a distraught woman, sobbing and howling into the approaching night. Blood drained from my face and I damn near lost control of my bladder, listening to that witchy cry. It was filled with a kind of wickedness that turned hope to rot. The kind of wickedness that you only see in the movies or read about in books. Before my mind could talk some sense into my churning guts, I took off running over rocks and roots not even looking where I was fleeing, just desperate to escape that wickedly inhuman scream.

However, it seemed as though no matter how swiftly I pushed my legs past snarled thickets and muddy ditch runoff, nearly twisting my bad ankle twice, those strange and uneven footsteps kept pounding after me from behind. I swore that whatever it was had been purposefully snapping whole saplings like twigs just to torment me as it hounded me like easy prey through gullies and briar patches for over a mile straight. I kept trying to glance back quickly over my shoulder whenever I thought that I had gained some ground, but whenever I did I would catch some blur of writhing shadows shifting through distant tree trunks, always closer than seemed possible. Whatever it was that pursued me carried with it the heavy, rotten smells of roadkill and bad eggs. There came a point when I felt something nipping at my heels and the smell was so overpowering that for a moment I honestly thought that I would pass out. I started screaming for help, knowing fully well that there was no one around to hear me out there. The creature was obviously aiming to tire me out inch by inch with relentless pursuit into places so wild that it seemed like none of it had ever been touched by humanity before I so rudely trespassed there.  In what felt like hours later, I just smashed bodily into this huge web of white birch trees bent and woven together by past storms so dense I couldn't hope to bust through their clawed branches. It was only then, when I thought I had finally found a second to just breathe for a moment, that the deep gouge marks in the maple trees came back to me. Sobbing, I spun around, with my back pressed to those peeling tree trunks, also with deep gouge marks in them that had to have been created by something incredibly strong, finally ready to face the thing at last. I decided to give up my flight and as soon as I made that decision, it seems like whatever was pursuing me also gave up because the chase sounds stopped just as abruptly.

I couldn't see the black shape darting between the gnarled pines anymore and I heard absolutely nothing at all. Throughout the entire forest it seemed like I was the only living creature, along with my relentless pursuer of course. My chest was burning fiercely from so much running and I gasped in breaths that seemed too loud for the silence. The woods appeared to be holding its own breath with me. That nice cool fall breeze turned sharp and icy, and all the hair raised up stiff on the back of my neck as I scanned for signs of the lurking thing. It wasn't over yet! Everything got so silent I worried blood was pounding too loud in my ears to notice it sneaking up on me. Then slowly, I noticed a creepy, almost human-looking silhouette starting to stretch impossibly thin from the shadows between two skinny jack pines, facing my direction. It stayed hunched down at first so I couldn't see any details, just that its fuzzy outline was darker than anything I ever seen - like a cutout of the deepest and most hidden parts of a cave. As it started to straighten, I could just tell this shadow was incredibly-abnormally tall and skinny, and it was swaying a little. It didn't seem to have any eyes or mouth that I could see, until it turned its long angular head my way and I realized it had a full rack of huge branchy antlers crowning its wraith-like head. When it rippled and took a couple limping steps out of the pines toward me, kind of continental-like, It began stretching its freaky spindly arms wide. It had extra joints, and then it opened its mouth and I swear it let out that same spine-shivering shriek as I had heard earlier. I realized it was angry, but I don't really know how I knew that. I had no frame of reference for how this thing looked normally but I was as sure of it as I was my own name. I had severely pissed this thing off, somehow. The scream felt like it turned my bones to jelly and almost made my ears bleed. It was so piercing. That thing wasn't natural at all, obviously and it was more like it was a demon from hell than anything that belonged on this earthly realm. It could have come there straight from hell or, more than likely, someplace much, much worse. As another unearthly screech rang out, I screamed as loudly as I could and kept screaming as I turned to claw my way out of the wicked birch branches I had somehow and quite suddenly become entangled in. I didn't care at all about the bark scratching angry lines across my cheeks as I fumbled and tumbled my way through them as fast as humanly possible. I just needed to get away from whatever the hell that thing was. It wanted to consume me and it was hungry. Those two things were all I knew for certain at that point. I could feel that shadow watching me from the dark the whole way as I ran for my damn life, for my soul, from those possessed woods.

By the time I stumbled bloody and crying onto the park road where some random truck found me two miles south as I staggered half out of my mind towards town, I couldn't hardly even whisper the word water. My throat was so shredded raw from screaming in fear and sobbing uncontrollably. I tried my best to tell the stranger who picked me up and took mercy on me about the monstrous, demonic thing that chased me through the woods and how it was seemingly straight out of some nightmare place, but he didn't seem to want to hear any of it and I think he initially thought I was high on drugs or drunk or something. He told me that I must've just gotten turned around off-trail and that maybe I had mistaken some ordinary animal, a buck perhaps. He then began to insinuate that I had merely been spooked by nothing more than mere shadows and then told me that's why women don't belong alone in the woods. He drove me to the police station where I thought I would fill out a report and they would go in search of the demonic beast. That's not what happened though and they treated me no better than the stranger and said almost the exact same things as he had. Like I said from the beginning it doesn't matter to me who believes me anymore and I don't care how crazy I sound. I try to warn anyone who will listen about it but since it happened my life has been a loving hell because everyone keeps looking at me like they feel bad for me. Like I'm crazy or something. But I know that evil thing is still lurking in those woods, hungry and waiting. Whatever it was had been intelligent enough that it was taking its time and purposely doing things to terrify me, as though it were all some part of the thrill of the hunt for it or something. I tried to insist that the police warn the public so that hunters and little kids who play out there, just as I had when I was younger, would be prepared or better yet stay out altogether. I know I will never go into those woods again and I truly believe that it wasn't alone in that forest and that it isn't alone on this planet. I fear that somehow the others would know who I was, somehow, and that the moment I step foot into the woods again, alone, or otherwise, it would finish what the other had started.

# STORY 10

I always considered the forests of Michigan my sanctuary, a place where the whispers of nature drowned out the clamor of city life. That was until the autumn of 2018, when the woods revealed a hidden, sinister facet.

It started as a typical hike. The leaves, painted with fiery hues, crunched under my boots, and the crisp air filled my lungs. As evening approached, a feeling of unease crept over me. It wasn't uncommon to hear stories of dogmen, mythical creatures said to roam these parts. I'd always shrugged them off as tall tales, but that day, a distant rustling in the underbrush set my nerves on edge. The sound seemed to follow me, just out of sight. I quickened my pace, attributing the noise to a curious animal, possibly a fox or, in the worst case, a coyote.

The forest grew darker, and the rustling intensified, closer now. My heart raced; I could almost sense the presence of something large and alive, moving parallel to my path. The dogman legend flashed in my mind. I envisioned a creature of nightmares, a bipedal being with the head of a canine and the body of a man. A cold sweat broke out across my brow.

But what emerged from the shadows was far more horrifying than any dogman. The creature that stood before me was a grotesque parody of a human being. Towering, it stood at least eight feet tall, its skin pale and stretched taut over protruding bones. Its eyes, sunken in their sockets, glowed with a malevolent light. The Wendigo, as I would later come to know it, had antlers that branched off its head like twisted, leafless trees. Its mouth, too large for its emaciated face, was filled with jagged teeth, stained with what looked disturbingly like dried blood.

I was paralyzed with fear, my breath coming in short, sharp gasps. The creature tilted its head, as if curious, then let out a guttural growl that seemed to shake the very ground beneath me. I knew I should run, but my legs wouldn't obey. It was as though the Wendigo's gaze had rooted me to the spot.

Time seemed to slow as it took a step towards me, its movements unnaturally fluid. The stories I'd heard of the Wendigo spoke of a creature born from cannibalism, a spirit of the forest turned malevolent, hungering eternally for human flesh. It was said to be a harbinger of death, and in that moment, I believed it.

But then, as quickly as it had appeared, the creature recoiled. A distant howl, perhaps from a real coyote or wolf, echoed through the forest, and the Wendigo turned its head sharply towards the sound. That moment of distraction was all I needed. My legs found their strength, and I ran as though the devil himself were at my heels.

I didn't stop running until I burst out of the tree line and into the safety of my car. I drove home with shaking hands, glancing repeatedly in the rearview mirror, half expecting to see those haunting, glowing eyes following me.

I haven't returned to the forest since that night. The memories haunt me, a constant reminder of the creature that lurks in the shadows of Michigan's woods. I know

now that some legends are rooted in terrifying truths, and that some horrors are all too real.

# STORY 11

As a recently divorced empty-nester, I jumped at my sister's offer to join her on a work trip to quaint Prince Edward Island. I'd always longed to visit the tranquil beaches, cozy cottages, and fertile emerald fields of Canada's tiny green isle floating off the east coast. But nestled within those postcard fishing harbors and rolling dunes lurked a sinister presence...an eternal predator not found on any tourist map. In my eagerness, I trespassed straight into the territorial hunting grounds of the man-eating phantom called the Wendigo.

Jet lagged upon arriving at our cottage lodging near whispering woodlands, I asked the kindly local host about nearby nature trails to settle my nerves. Unease flashed across his eyes momentarily before he pointed me to a nearby valley brimming with wild forest secluded from the village's manicured trails. I now know why he kept multiple tall fences encircling his charming property which looked strangely out of place when everything else exuded quaint island hospitality. If only I had understood then that those barricades confined a different sort of guest on PEI...one who comes without invitation.

Enchanted by the valley's raw beauty as dusk settled, I dismissed the host's peculiar reluctance for me to enter the dense woods alone. Birds filled the chilled autumn air with songs of farewell to the fading light while my senses drank deep of nature's fragile peace tinged with decay. In my reverie I almost missed the foreign odor riding the breezes...like a breath from open graves.

Unease slithered up my spine as I scanned for large animals through ever-darkening brush. Then a shrill cry exploded from the shadows that clenched my heart - the sound of a fiend claiming new prey. Guttural bellows shook the high canopy as immense footfalls crashed nearer from the gloom. I stumbled backwards when a shape hurtled from the pines, far too tall and lean...and so wrongfully fast. My skin prickled at the creature's smell of fungi and putrid meat. Cold terror clutched me in its talons...this was no ordinary animal. I had naively wandered into the hunting ground of accursed legends. Towering before me with antlers splitting the night and eyes smoldering like red cinders floated the phantom terror of Mi'kmaq tales. I had awakened the insatiable Wendigo!

I gaped in disbelief at the emaciated giant, its withered flesh patched gray and yellow barely masking its skeletal frame. Jagged fangs jutted from a lipless maw below flared nostrils, while each claw tapered to gnarled points meant to tear open screaming victims. Most disturbingly, recognition flickered in those red-coal eyes...the ageless cunning of a supreme predator.

My mind froze as atavistic alarms shrieked. I knew its slightest touch meant agonizing death. When the beast flashed a rictus grin of welcome, I screamed soundlessly. This wasn't some decomposing zombie but an eternal spirit summoned by native curses, unbound by modern laws to feast upon mankind alone. All I could do was screech breathlessly and flee that primal horror marking me as its next meal.

Crashing wildly through whipping trees and clawing briars, I felt inhuman talons knife past again and again trying to take me down as the frenzied Wendigo gave chase with preternatural speed. Panicked glances revealed the gangly fiend easily keeping pace, toying cat-like even as it herded me deeper into its domain. I cried out for mercy until hoarse, hearing only the monster's guttural bark in response...like the mocking laughter of Death itself.

My strength evaporated during that tortuous flight through stygian woodlands. Just as hope died of escaping the Wendigo's clutches, distant lights appeared between the gnarled oaks still leagues ahead. Spying that glowing refuge, instincts took over as I scrambled on hands and knees toward the village's outermost homes. A mere dozen yards from precious salvation, searing talons sliced my leg numb even as a deafening roar of victory paralyzed my soul.

I flopped limply to face grinning jaws as the emaciated beast crouched to claim its prize. Glowing eyes narrowed at the lamp-lit houses daring it closer as the fiend bristled with rage for lost prey. My heart leapt seeing the Wendigo thwarted so near my very salvation! With an earsplitting shriek that set neighborhood dogs howling, the gangly monster melted into the darkness.

The petrified host reacted violently to seeing his protective charms breached when I appeared bloody and half-feral on his porch. Screaming myths had turned real, he needed to safeguard his people against further

Wendigo attacks! My sister flew us off PEI at dawn, fearing township retaliation as eccentric foreigners who brought released evil among innocent and devout communities.

I dare not guess if Prince Edward Island only knows fleeting peace. For I glimpsed eternity burning in those malevolent Wendigo eyes beyond reason or death...an incarnation of doom itself prowling the island's forgotten places under shadowy boughs. And it yet hungers for my soul.

# STORY 12

I decided that I needed to get what happened to me last week down in writing before I forget most of it and what better way to make sure the experience doesn't become nothing more than a bizarre memory than to put it out there for all to see and make sure I get every detail correct while it's all fresh in my mind. It happened while I was at work, on an otherwise typical day, and many of the details already elude me. I feel like I should preface this by saying that the paranormal isn't something I really think about so I honestly never knew if I was a believer or not and it's not something that normally comes up in conversations either. However, the answer to that question- whether or not I believe in the paranormal, after what happened to me last week, is most definitely a yes and I honestly feel like this isn't over and that it's something I will be exploring more of in the near future. I will obviously have to think about it because the whole experience was absolutely terrifying but I feel like if there's things like what I was confronted and came face to face with, during the day no less, out there in that isolated area of a well-known forest, then there has to be more and I don't know that I will be content to just leave it at that. That morning's dawn patrol started like any other crisp fall day keeping watch over miles of mountainous state parkland from my remote forest service station. I sipped bitter coffee while the clean and clear light of the sunrise filtered through firs fringing my gravel driveway, as I made a mental note of all of the overgrown trail sections due for maintenance. I headed out on the 30 minute drive to our region's fire lookout. I got a message from my immediate supervisor that I needed to check on an old maintenance shed and restock supplies. The area I was headed to was by an isolated tower that I went out and checked or restocked a few times each season. I didn't mind, and in fact I welcomed the long, winding trek up into fragrant cedars shielding the lookout's lofty nest on a peaceful Thursday. However, this time something was immediately different and from the moment I locked the truck and glanced upwards through gently swaying boughs to see that still, glassy booth with the northern mountains behind it, my lungs cinched uneasily. Thomas, a coworker of mine would already be out there, as he was the one who had been manning a nearby station overnight and I was told to let him know I was there before I did anything. He also knew the procedure for sighting midweek patrols and he was. Most of the time, waving a red kerchief from the railing as soon as vehicles approached below. However, no vibrant flag or white-haired sentry greeted me that cloudless morning.

I called the lookout's direct line from my truck first, letting it ring out the longest protocol while studying the sturdy iron staircase. It appeared intact and clear of debris following recent storms. Clicking my radio off annoyed, I assured myself Thomas likely just wandered deeper into the evergreen stands seeking better sunrise vistas to photograph as was his hobby. Many times, I had come upon him chatting with blue jays as eccentric old foresters tend to, losing track of patroller arrival time. At least nothing seemed overtly amiss from my spot squinting up the tower's sheer west face. But when I grabbed my personal gear bag and moved closer for a proper inspection, my clammy hands registered what my calm mind initially dismissed as routine maintenance needs. There, marring the weathered plank steps near my eye level, began a series of deep parallel grooves running vertically down the ladder's left side. Splintered furrows resembling claw marks or maybe coarse filing gouged furiously across three wooden steps in that narrow track. I brushed trembling fingers over the gashes feeling how they channeled almost an inch into solid cedar. No animal should be able to tear seasoned timber with such singular force. The savage precision of those slices stirred the fine hairs on my neck as I spun around to survey the surrounding woods. All seemed still, except for some crows cawing a rude interruption from upslope. At that moment though, the forest's calm felt dangerously muted. With no wind to shift and branches, I detected a strange absence of smaller fidgeting life usually busying about the understory. Not one scurrying squirrel or glimpses of mule deer amongst terrain they've freely roamed for generations and that I had never not seen while there myself. Was this unnatural hush somehow connected to Thomas's unprecedented absence as well?

Fighting a rigid spine, I forced myself up the creaking

steps so that I could make sure that the old veteran wasn't inside, maybe incapacitated or having had some other tragedy befall him. He was elderly, after all, and I considered him a friend and therefore knew more than most of the other people we worked with about some of his more difficult health struggles. Suddenly the thought came to me that perhaps whatever had made those marks in the ladder had gotten to him and harmed or injured him somehow and I had to force myself to press on up the stairs, worrying that whatever it was would still be there when I opened the door, possibly startling it. I reached the reinforced hatch winded more from anxiety than exertion, calling ahead is protocol when approaching any forest service structure so as not to startle occupants. I yelled out again but when I received no answer for the third time, I opened the door slowly and carefully and then let myself in. The heavy door swung open smoothly as I blinked, adjusting to indoor dim. Through the single pane windows, open blue sky framed still mountains beyond like one of the picturesque scenes in a calendar of landscapes that hung nearby. Everything appeared tidy per Thomas's disciplined nature that rivaled military precision despite this isolated outpost being his self-imposed retirement refuge. His regulation cot lay crisply made with a thermal blanket folded square. Dog-eared wildlife books and crumbling maps proved recently handled and eagerly referenced alongside cracked mugs near the small Coleman camp stove. Thomas's precious anthology series that he was always reading lay open atop scattered pencils and a handwritten letter I shouldn't have read referencing his niece's upcoming visit. Guilt flushed my face, though her presence confirmed my early assumption that Thomas wouldn't simply abandon his passion project cataloging alpine denizens without good cause.

The only true oddity blaring from that peaceful scene was Thomas's favorite Kodak camera sitting discarded by the far bench below a cracked window. My throat pinched at the careless treatment so counter to his typical delicate ritual with the antiquated device. Something profoundly alarming must have drawn the lanky photographer quickly away without proper prepara-tions. I rushed towards flakes of shattered glass hoping to glean some clue outside, only to find his rifle still secured near the exit hatch rather than its usual post by Thomas's elbow, where he always kept it while gazing out at prime wildlife vistas. He considered the well-maintained firearm mere insurance against problematic predators, though I understood its deeper comfort honoring a young ranger's loss against fateful odds two decades prior. Finding it abandoned rocked my core with certainty that animal cunning certainly wasn't what snatched Thomas from his lair this crisp autumnal dawn.

No fierce buck or capacious bear could have accomplished such a neat and stealthy removal of a whole human being. Not to mention he was a war vet and wouldn't have just easily gone anywhere. Not with anyone or anything. My ears were ringing and my pulse was pounding as I descended back down the stairs, worried about Thomas but having no more answers than I had when I initially arrived there and found his post abandoned in the first place. I radioed headquarters and insisted that something was wrong at Thomas' post and requested corroborating reports from the neighboring lookout towers. I was already geared up to start a full scale search to find the old man and make sure that he was okay and not in need of any assistance. However, static cut the line mid-sentence, leaving me silently scanning three hundred and sixty degrees around my truck feeling scrutinized by a presence cunning enough to block communications. Could that really be the case though, or was my imagination, the situation as a whole and the isolation of the area just causing me to be irrational. I felt like I was being watched, that was for certain, but the thought that some supernatural force had cut my communication with headquarters startled me. I leaned heavily against the sun-soaked driver door when a branch crack echoed from the narrow back country road I arrived by. The noise ricocheted off escarpment walls that seemed to press closer as I waited desperately for Thomas to call out or come limping around the bend. Instead, the sinewy form of what looked like a barefoot man wavered gradually into view downhill, where the light wasn't quite shining just yet. Even at around three hundred yards away, details were disturbingly unusual instead of reassuring me and providing me with the relief I had expected.

The figure appeared shirtless and freakishly gaunt, swaying unsteadily as if suspended by taut strings. Rubbery limbs jutting too far from its torso seemed to dislocate further when it bobbed rapidly and erratically towards my immobilized patrol truck. The emaciated head lacked distinguishing features beyond a lipless gash vaguely resembling a yawning mouth. Somehow still though, the skeletal being stared, faceless from deep sockets, directly into me from 80 yards uphill and quickly closing in on me. Trapped by that eyeless scrutiny, my full faculties returned only when it jerkily lunged to cross half the ravine in a single gangly stride. I'll admit it- I screamed like a terrified woman and I almost dove for my driver-side door as claw-tipped fingers grabbed the air just inches away from my neck. Peeling backwards, I quickly and almost instinctively reversed and as I did so I bashed limbs on the steering column and twisted my keys in the ignition. A rear tire narrowly missed the shrieking creature as I floored it into a nearby clearing. With my heart beating so loudly it seemed to be all I could hear, I radioed for emergency air support. I was absolutely frenzied and unable to get out the right words to express what it was that I had witnessed and what I needed from them. I wanted backup in the form of lethal force as I was convinced down to the marrow of my bones that the pale creature would continue pursuing me for as long and as far as its spindly crawling limbs allowed it to once I abandoned my barricaded truck to flee this cursed watch zone. You see, I had missed the clearing, narrowly, and slammed my truck into the tower itself. I had hit it with such force that it nearly crumpled my front end and I knew I had to get out and make a run for it before that creature got a hold of me and it wasn't until just before sundown that anyone found me.

Right near some boulder fields, as I made my way for the fifth time down a steep embankment, still trying to outrun the strange and malevolent creature that by now I was convinced had done something terrible to my friend Thomas, a rescue pilot observed my collapse in a dusty gully. I had been running and stopping, hiding, and ducking, all in an attempt to evade the strange, pale creature that pursued me through those eerily quiet woods for nearly twelve hours and I had collapsed due to exhaustion and dehydration. I think my intense fear had something to do with it as well and right before I collapsed I remember thinking that I was going to die out there but I thought I would become a victim of the pale creature and didn't even consider what I was putting my body through. Could someone die of fright? It's possible and I believe I came very close to doing just that in this situation. I didn't wake up until two full days later, and when I did I was in the hospital with restraints on my wrists. Thomas visited kindly beside his niece, Millie, at my bedside. Once she wiped my delirious tears, I still couldn't believe that I was alive or that any of it had actually happened, he finally told me where he had been and what had happened to him that day too. It was all very mundane but what I want to tell you about now is what he confided in me next. He recounted a terrifying experience with what he hesitantly named the "starvation demon" from his days long ago in the military, His "greenhorn days" he called them. That encounter happened in the nineteen sixties and when he notified the police they immediately dismissed it as the ramblings of a man suffering from sleeplessness and exhaustion, who had a hallucination due to being over-worked and overstressed. He managed to let it go and convince himself that they were probably right and that he hadn't actually experienced what he thought he did-that being a grayish pale being that looked very similar based on his description to what I knew I had just seen. He didn't think of it much after a few months had passed and he managed to get back to his normal life, for the most part. However, finding me driven to madness mirroring his long-buried memories proved too eerie to ignore anymore.

He thought he knew where the marks in the ladder had come from and so he headed out to perform a cursory search of the area. Because he was so startled by what he was seeing, he hadn't wanted to bring his firearm with him, for fear he would use it recklessly and injure some innocent bystander or something. He heard me call out to him, once, but by the time he made it back to the tower he saw my truck smashed up into it and I was nowhere to be found. He called for help. I told him my story, only verifying what he felt he already knew and it was enough for him to finally retire. He gave two weeks' notice but I've not gone a single day without speaking to him since all of this happened and he said he can never be comfortable out there again and he's horrified that his original experience had been true in the first place, knowing he had built his whole life and especially his career on a lie that wasn't a lie at all. While Thomas was always friendly enough, we hadn't ever really gotten to know one another in all the years we've worked together but that's since changed and I feel like he's now a part of my extended family. We don't always talk about the entity when we speak but sometimes we do and he's been doing his best to convince me to "just leave well enough alone." I don't know if I can do that, not even for Thomas, who- for all intents and purposes, probably saved my life and got me out of the clutches of that pale, ghoulish entity that had me in its sights for an entire half of a day. The thing didn't even look strong enough to be able to carry out such a relentless pursuit and yet it did. In the little bit of research, I've managed to do since this all happened, I learned that for the people native to the area and most of the locals too, those woods in particular hold indiscriminate danger for people who aren't willing to respect the legends. However, that makes little sense to me because how can you disrespect something you aren't aware is there? I fully intend on doing a lot more research into the legends surrounding that forest in particular and all of the ancient creatures, malevolent and otherwise, allegedly inhabiting it as well.

If I should come across anything else that would be considered paranormal, one way or the other, I'll be sure to send that story in as well. My superiors keep hounding me to send in a formal statement but I haven't been able to do so yet because I think that lying about what I saw and my experience that day could be very dangerous for the other people who work in that same field as me, especially those from the same unit and out of the same headquarters. However, Thomas said I need to pick my battles, and also, that I need to choose wisely who I tell the truth to. It could end up costing me more than my reputation should I reveal what I saw and the truth about what happened to me out there that day to the wrong person. It's interesting advice for sure, I am just still struggling with it. Thanks for letting me get this down while it's all fresh and for allowing me to share my story with other people.

# STORY 13

I always have trouble when telling people about what I experienced as far as the paranormal because people nowadays believe that the entity I encountered is either just a story that someone made up and put online, specifically called a "creepypasta" or, they believe that it's a tulpa. A tulpa is, in its most basic definition, a being or creature- an entity of sorts, that has been created somehow but that was brought to life due to a very large number of the collective believing in it as reality. For example, in the paranormal community many people believe the black eyed kids are tulpas and that the journalist who first mentioned them simply had a scary idea for a story but that it was so believable for so many people, those people believed in it enough that it became a real phenomenon. I hope that explains what a tulpa is but more importantly I am here to tell you that the entity I encountered is neither a tulpa nor is it a so-called creepypasta. It's a real being and it's pure malevolence. It's something I grew up hearing about, long before the internet even existed. People don't really believe in the Slender Man anymore, at least not folks who didn't grow up swallowed by deep forests where old fears linger like smoke trapped under a blanket of pine needles. Like I said, from what I understand, they claim he's just some internet scary story gone viral to spook kids. But I know the hideous truth after what my cousin and I saw at my family's old hunting cabin many years ago, during a particularly cold and rough winter. That towering shadow haunting the northern Wisconsin woods since before my grandfather's time is as real as the antlers decorating our knotty log walls...and it seems as though it might be coming back and trying to steal one of my relatives away as payment for the fact it didn't get its hands on several members of my family throughout the years who have come into close contact with it.

I had been in college for a year without coming home much so when Christmas rolled around I figured it would be nice, for old time's sake, to go and spend it at the cabin with the rest of my family. I was looking forward to seeing my family and most of my cousins would also be there. My aunt Sheila, who was my favorite aunt, would be there with her daughter Anna, who she spoiled rotten but who was still a good kid, and her husband, my uncle Nate. A few other family members would be there too, as well as my parents. Aunt Sheila lived a twelve hour drive away from me, in the city in Chicago, and I really was excited to see her. Because she had spoiled Anna so much and basically treated her like a princess in the city, she told me she was hoping that the isolated cabin would somehow toughen her up before she headed to college out east. I agreed to go but it isn't really like I completely had a choice as my mother and aunt Sheila were sisters and they were both masters of manipulation and guilt tripping, and so I agreed to not only make an appearance but to stay and be a part of the festivities with the rest of my family. I got there just as aunt Sheila, Anna and Uncle Nate pulled up and I excitedly got out of the car to greet them. I was nervous from the drive, and just happy not to be alone anymore. The five hour trip went smooth until that last winding leg off the rural highway onto the icy dirt road leading to our century-old cabin 20 miles into a somewhat well-known national forest. At least it was well known for the area. The sight of those familiar snow-heaped woods pressing close up against the car in all directions made me suddenly nervous and an instinctual unease hit me as I started to remember, as soon as the tree branches started darkening the woods around me, as they blotted out the setting sun in the sky, a story that the older people in my family told us kids from a very young age about something that had allegedly happened to my grandfather and his brother, decades earlier. The woods around the cabin always made me uncomfortable after that. It reminded me that I wasn't imagining things when the woods went silent, and I couldn't hear a thing as I passed the Forest Service's 5-mile marker into that gloomy maze of timber that led to the cabin. My uncle Nate had always told us that even the animals still shunned this area after whatever it was that had happened to my grandfather and his brother Logan, but it was always such a vague and unfinished story that made me scared as a kid. As I got older I just thought it was something they told us to keep us from wandering too far into the woods. I only knew that whatever it was had happened past the last bend that overlooked the now frozen creek.

Even according to local legends though, there was

allegedly an evil that lurked in that area that many people claimed to have seen with their own eyes. I tried not to think about it and turned my radio up, blasting my homemade mixtape in my ears to shush my mind up about it. I knew all of the older cousins, Anna included, knew the story but they only knew as much as I did, which was enough for me and I had no interest in knowing more. That was mainly because I knew how scared I always felt in that particular area, whether we were driving through to get to the cabin as we were then or walking through as kids and playing in the woods surrounding that spot. It always felt different, and not in a good way. Local legends say that some sort of malevolent presence haunts that land, starving animals and putting a chill in men's hearts. Our clan learned to keep moose rifles loaded when forced to travel through or work timber back there, at least back in the fifties. As I gathered my things out of the car and started heading into the cabin to get myself settled and relaxed, my uncle grabbed my shoulder, hard. I turned around and he looked me dead in the eye and told me in no uncertain terms that if I caught myself or Anna wandering alone past where that frozen creek was, at the foot of the old waterfall, that I needed to get us back to the cabin as quickly as possible. It was the strangest thing. However, I did remember that, as kids, we were always warned to stay away from that area and if we did find ourselves in it, we were to immediately turn around and go directly back to the cabin. We all knew better from a very young age not to pass by that waterfall or to go any further into the woods than it. I assured him I would take care of Anna but I was annoyed by his reminder, thinking that surely she was old enough now, and had been for a while to keep an eye on herself. But, being the older cousin, I figured I could keep an eye out for her. After all, they visited the cabin a lot more than I did and maybe something had happened there that I didn't know about and Uncle Nate just wanted to assure it didn't happen again. Anna was spoiled rotten but she looked up to me and normally she listened to what I had to say, even if reluctantly.

Anna must have heard what her father said to me because she rolled her eyes rebelliously and pushed past him roughly, walking up the stairs and into the cabin. I helped him grab her bags and we went inside as well, with Aunt Sheila following closely behind us. We all got our things unpacked and set up in our respective rooms, with Anna and I sharing a room with two other cousins who weren't there yet, and the adults doing their own thing and then we waited for everyone else to show up. I decided then to make more effort reconnecting Anna with nature's lessons and our clan history on this trip, knowing that her parents both knew I wouldn't let anything happen to her and I phrased it in a way to her like we were going to be hanging out together for the whole trip. She was thrilled but I was just trying to get her to trust me so that I could teach her a lesson about respect. Not only in respecting traditions but also, just respecting the elder people in our family in general. Eventually everyone showed up and said hello to everyone else and we all settled in for a relaxing evening in front of the cozy living room hearth. Everyone but Anna, that is. She decided her time was better spent in the kitchen, causing a ruckus, and shrieking about imagined mouse droppings in there.

Eventually she joined the rest of the family though and as she did, our uncle Wyatt was in the middle of proudly displaying the mounted twelve-point buck head he bagged earlier before passing a whiskey flask to Uncle Nate. I wasn't paying attention and instead I focused on Anna, who was tucked anxiously between her bickering parents on our squeaking moose leather couch, the firelight illuminating her delicate features. She faked aloof teen annoyance well, but I sensed her attention lingering on the rifle display above the mantle rather than anything else. So, I cleared my throat and began retelling how our grandfather had stayed snowed in here alone one long December week back in 1957 when the roads were still all dirt and motor cabins were rarer than paved highways. Suddenly my uncle Nate must've suddenly become extra defensive from fatigue and drink by then because my modest ghost story soon sparked a full blown familial clash over whether to perpetuate our clan's "irrational rural traditions" or let the old ways fade as we modernized. Caught in the middle, I felt honor-bound to remind my well-off elders what modern arrogance made them blind to in those brooding woods. But I also worried I'd only frighten my impressionable young cousin rather than instruct her. I really wanted her to be okay. Her parents were so cool, but she had been "a miracle baby" and was always treated like the golden child in the family. Life in college would not be kind to her and even if it was, the real world wouldn't be. I knew my aunt Sheila hated how her daughter behaved most of the time or at the very least I knew she was embarrassed by it and it was my love for her and Uncle Nate that made me so adamant with myself about turning Anna right. So as Nate and Sheila's bickering escalated, I moved quietly to sit by Anna's knee and asked if she'd like to hear the special tale Granddad told Uncle Logan near the end. Anna bit her lip but nodded, skillfully dodging her mom's scolding grasp to slide down by the warm hearthstones with me.

Settling cross-legged to face each other, I lowered my voice respectfully, and started telling Anna how Grandpa Lorne, our mother's father, and the patriarch of our crazy bunch, encountered a hungry spirit when he was just my age back during the Great Depression. Times were tough and game was hard to come by, so Lorne often broke laws poaching crown land so his family could eat. One bitterly cold December dusk trekking back from illegal traplines towards the homestead, grandpa swore he felt something tall and invisible stalking him between the gloomy pines. An instinctual dread he never forgot sank its claws in as the then-nameless entity followed him relentlessly for miles, its presence leaching away all sound from the frozen forest. Just when the starving teen feared he would collapse in the deep snow, moonlight revealed a clearing where the familiar cabin crouched welcoming with our grandmother, Ida- his mother- visible stoking a hearty fire inside. New strength flooded Lorne's aching legs as he raced desperately for that golden glow while the unseen predator kept pace, never quite catching hold of him but almost in a constant and relentless pursuit instead. Grandpa dove gasping past the blessed iron gate that led to the front steps, all the while feeling the ancient thing halt furiously just beyond it. The next day Ida discovered that some of Lorne's homemade statues, which he called "Wards" back then, had been ripped to shreds and torn apart, as though they had been made by paper and not steel, like they were. Our grandfather had always had what the family called "a second sight" and he was always making these talis- mans, some tiny and others large like statues, and gifting them to family members. Mostly though, he set them outside, all over the property where he lived with his mother, father, and siblings. He said it kept the evil away, and no one questioned him. Once Ida summoned the courage to tell Lorne about what happened to his talismans, he warned her against ever roaming the forest on moonless nights, and she in turn warned his siblings. That's where that rule in our family came from. Anna smiled at me because she knew that warning well, we had all grown up hearing it.

She wanted to hear more and I could see that I was getting through to her and she was starting to become excited about being there with us and so I told her about local legends of people going missing in the woods on moonless nights and just in general and by the end of it we were laughing and the adults had all gone off somewhere else, probably to their respective beds or outside on the back deck to hang out and reminisce themselves. It would be another day or two before our other cousins got there and so we decided to stick together. So basically everyone from that night on with my grandfather, and not only in our family, knew to stay out of the woods at night in general but especially when there was no moon and there are decades of stories in the local area of people who didn't heed that message and paid the price for it but I could see that she was becoming scared and so I decided to change the subject and we went into our room to look through magazines together, planning on taking a walk through the woods the following afternoon to talk and reconnect. I knew that something had happened near that waterfall, or just past it, to our grandfather's younger brother, who we referred to as Uncle Logan, but I didn't know what and so I just casually reminded Anna that we needed to be back by dark and not go past the waterfall. She agreed and that was that.

I feel the need to justify my building this story up so much before getting to the initial point but I think it's important that people understand the history of the area and my family before I move on. Now that you all have a feel for that, let me continue. Anna and I were up bright and early and we left for our hike at around two in the afternoon. We knew it would be getting dark around five and so we promised to be back long before then. We walked for about an hour and suddenly came to the frozen waterfall. Anna froze in place and stared at it and I knew she was feeling the same sense of menace and foreboding as I was at the sight of it. I asked if she wanted to go back to the cabin but she said she suddenly felt very dizzy and needed to sit down for a few minutes. I noticed I was getting a searing, severe pain behind one of my eyes that was making my vision blurry and so I agreed with her that we needed to sit, even though I didn't tell her how I was feeling. We just sat there in silence and stared at the waterfall and it was like we had gone into some sort of trance because the next thing either of us remembered was that it was suddenly almost dark outside. It was like we blinked and some outside force had fast forwarded a clock and it was dusk outside suddenly. Anna still wasn't feeling well and we were both very disoriented. I started to walk back to the cabin but she was making her way towards the waterfall. I called for her to stop but she didn't listen and it seemed like she was being pulled along by some unseen force. I followed her and figured there was no time like the present to prove all the superstitions wrong or at least see for us what was out there, beyond the waterfall. We walked cloaked in darkness by the trees but the sun was still peeking through them a bit. Suddenly though everything went quiet and Anna said her head wasn't hurting anymore. I noticed my migraine was gone too. It was too quiet out there though and it was obvious to me that something wasn't quite right. I stopped and said I wanted to go back but saw a look on Anna's face that I will never forget. There was a statue that looked like it had been handmade from bent and welded steel and I was a little excited to see it because I knew it was one that our grandfather made when he was younger. It was one of the ones said to keep the darkness at bay. Charming- and creepy looking. I followed Anna's slack jawed expression and saw that there appeared to be an extremely tall but very thin shadow on the snowy ground in front of us, about five feet away, but it didn't seem to be attached to anything. I looked all around and so did Anna but there was nothing at all that seemed to match that one particular shadow and I got the feeling that we needed to leave, right then and without delay, and turned once again to run away. That's when Anna started screaming bloody murder.

I turned and looked and saw that the shadow itself was no longer a shadow but an entity all its own. Long, tentacle-like arms had popped out of the very tall frame that had originally been there and we could see it as a three dimensional figure now. It had a white face but no eyes or lips, no nose or other features and it looked like someone had taken an eraser and erased its features completely. There was a bit of a blur to the face but the arms that ended in sharp looking tendrils were even more concerning as they undulated back and forth, seemingly coming towards us from the entity and in the cold yet breezeless forest. There was nothing to account for the swaying except that the figure in front of us was moving its arms closer and closer to us. It was at least twelve feet tall and its legs were a bit thicker than its arms. It wasn't quite wearing a suit but I could see how someone would think that if they only saw a quick glimpse of it. We both ran as fast as we could out of that area and didn't look back until we got to the cabin again and had closed the doors behind us. Our whole family was in the living room and they all were silently staring at us when we came in panic stricken. I blurted out that we had gone past the waterfall and they all broke into a chorus or angry comments and remarks aimed at us. We went into our room and locked the door, refusing to go back out there until everyone calmed down. Finally, they did and we explained to them what they saw. Nate told us that's the same creature Logan and our grandfather had seen all those years ago and the same one our grandfather spent his life trying to ward off of the property, but he eventually only managed to keep it at bay, just beyond the waterfall. We were terrified but eventually everyone calmed down and we called it a night. Anna and I didn't get much sleep that night. All night long we heard tapping on the window of our bedroom but our other cousins who were now in the room with us didn't hear it and slept through it, even as it became much louder as the hours wore on. Neither of us wanted to look outside but eventually I couldn't take it anymore and I got up to look. I saw the same figure, who I now know to be Slenderman, standing in the middle of the huge yard, far away from our window, which was on the second floor, and from the cabin itself. I could see the tentacled arms reaching around and stretching to the window, as it knocked and tried to lure us out there.

My aunt gave me permission to drive Anna back to the city the following day and I stayed with her until they got home a few days later. We weren't as fearful with no woods around and eventually the Slenderman incident became nothing more than a memory. Recently though Anna had her first grandchild and she's having nightmares that the figure from the cabin is coming for the little girl. She explained she hadn't even thought of it in years and now she's terrified all the time but that her daughter won't listen to her about it and calls it dumb urban legends. She blames that on what the internet has done to the story. I didn't have much advice for her but tried to comfort her anyway as that night changed our relationship and we have been like sisters ever since. I don't know if the nightmares she's having are real or anything like that but I do know they're real to her and I also hope for her sake that they aren't real. And for the sake of that baby girl. Just because we call something an urban legend today doesn't mean that's what it is or what it always was and I've come to find out that many things considered to be urban legends actually have real history in some parts of the world and people believe that whatever it was actually existed at some point in time. The way I see it is, why take a chance? Be respectful to all the old legends you hear whether in your town or passed down throughout generations in your family. That way, if there is even an element of truth to it, you won't ever have to worry or live in fear. Thanks for letting me share.

# STORY 14

I still have no idea what the hell we saw that night, or what any of it means. I've asked myself the question "why me?" more times than I can count since it happened but lately I've been thinking about it differently. Maybe I was just in the wrong place at the wrong time and none of it had any meaning. The one thing it did do for me was lead me to my wife, who I met when I joined a group for paranormal witnesses. Yes, such things do exist but you have to keep an open mind, and you have to know where to look. It just seems so random. I remember it like it was yesterday and not two and a half decades ago. My best friends Mike and I were driving through the forest and towards the lake, as we had done several times in the many years of our friendship. We met in the second grade when he moved in across the street from me and we were inseparable from the first time he bullied me. I gave it right back to him and a brotherhood was born immediately. I remember mocking him because he was scared from the beginning. I was more skeptical than anything else. We used to go camping in the random wooded areas by where we lived and once we both got our licenses, we would explore actual camping areas and lakes, things like that. This place though, was one we hadn't been to before but had heard a lot about. I was telling him that the myths associated with the place, of the creatures and monsters and things in the woods, were just stupid small town myths. Mike had always believed in the paranormal and it was one thing I always hung over his head because I thought it was all nonsense. I reminded him that there had never been any legitimate reports of anything being out there and that there hadn't ever been any tangible proof either. I admit, as I said all of this, I was nervously glancing towards the rippling water and all around us. It was unusual for me to be as nervous as I was and I felt relieved I hadn't been driving because then it would have been obvious that I wasn't feeling as nonchalant as I was pretending to. As our rental canoe bounced noisily on top of his battered old Jeep, for some reason I was really becoming scared but I couldn't figure out why. I understand this now to be that my instincts were telling me to get the hell out of there and not to stick around or ever go back. However, back then, I was numb and ignorant to all of that and I just thought his fear was rubbing off on me. Besides, it's creepy out in the forest in the middle of the night when you're alone and isolated. No matter who you are or where you are. I was determined not to let it get to me.

This was an impromptu camping trip we had only decided to go on at the last minute when we got bored hanging around Mike's house with nothing to do. Mike looked over at me, asking if I was okay, and he had a smirk on his face as he did so. He knew me too well. He once again explained to me that he had heard about this place, and the legends attached to it, from the town drunk when he was working a double shift as a barback the week earlier. He said he knew that we needed to find time to explore it and see if there was anything to the legends and rumors. I thought to myself that his source for information made the whole thing even worse. "I asked him what the old man described to him but he was vague with his answer, smirking as he described some sort of what he called a "fish monster" to me. Ridiculous, I know. That's what I thought too but please, hear me out and keep reading. The only reason I had gone with him in the first place is because I knew better than to fight my best friend's compulsion once his imagination snagged hold of some new adventure, reasonable or not. Besides, we hadn't hung out nearly enough since Christmas and a chance to truly unplug sounded welcome before starting summer internships. We had managed to get into the same college and into the same dorm, even if not the same room but we didn't take the same courses or have the same dreams so the internships were finally putting an end to our hanging out all the time.  As Mike turned down an unmarked gravel path cutting toward waning sunshine, I resigned myself to humoring this excursion and to trying not to mock him too much. I was game to take it as seriously as he was, if for nothing else but to shut him up.

We had already driven a good forty five minutes into the woods to get to the lake and we had navigated questionable traction down steep embankments overlooking glassy waters tucked into the depths of this seemingly vacant and eerily isolated forest preserve. Untouched wilderness wrapped the scene under tall swaying pines and we had the whole place to ourselves. That didn't strike me as too odd though, as there were other places

in the area that weren't as deep in the woods and where the forest wasn't as dense and the terrain much less treacherous. I gotta admit, the extreme isolation had me freaking out a little bit, which is probably why I was so antsy and fidgety from the moment I laid eyes on the water. I got distracted and was very impressed at the killer private campsite Mike had discovered on some musty park office map that had been given to him, strangely enough, by the old drunk. Whoever the guy was- I knew his name but couldn't ever remember it- he said he spent many of his nights there, in the woods. He was more than likely homeless as well as dirty and drunk all the time but that's another story altogether. He told Mike a bunch of paranormal stories about supernatural creatures he had seen out there but like I said, the "fish monster" took the cake for me. It was hilarious.....
So why was I so nervous? Scraggly fingers of thorn brush curled from the hillsides ringing this hidden jewel as insects buzzed lazily over scattered lily pads offshore. It was a lot louder than I expected it to be but I guessed that because it seemed so untouched by humanity and everything was so overgrown, that the insects and animals had made it their own. They'd made it their home. When I expressed my delight at the private campsite Mike grinned proudly. We pulled over and unloaded our gear as the sun faded fast into the sky. There wasn't another soul in sight and suddenly, once we got out of

the car and started unloading everything and getting it all together, that wasn't such a welcome thing as I initially thought it would be. The idea of there being safety in numbers that I'd learned in kindergarten was suddenly hammering through my head. We scrambled to pitch two small tents facing the fairly large, glistening lake, their silhouettes soon reflected perfectly off the windless mirror of the water, with the towering trees nearby, just as the first stars started to emerge.

Gathering tinder under the swaying branches, I couldn't help scanning for monsters in playful expectation, almost disappointed to find no eldritch inhabitants except for the usual raccoons and gnats. Within twenty minutes, our fire crackled merrily and its flickering glow engulfed a small portion of our camp. Despite the stars being out, maybe due to the density of all the trees that encircled us, it seemed pitch black outside other than the glow of those embers. As Mike and I pulled out some collapsible rods I playfully nudged him and wondered out loud if perhaps the fish man or fish monster as he called it would get upset that we were going to be poaching its trout out of the lake. My earlier reluctance, and anxiety, was replaced fully by a carefree and adventurous spirit. I hardly noticed the pale amber orb cresting over some distant pines and coming right for us until Mike nudged me eagerly, pointing out sparkles of what I thought were foxfire wisps moving all around in the underbrush across the shore from where we sat. Mike was excited about it and seemed almost childlike as he exclaimed that the forest really was magic! Just for the record, we didn't drink. Mike had grown up in a household that was destroyed by alcohol and drugs and so he didn't partake and felt strongly about being around any of the stuff. That was just fine with me because it wasn't really what I was into either. But I felt it necessary to say that. What he was feeling was the exhilaration of seeing nature in all her glory. Or so we thought. He started reminiscing about all the times we would camp by our house and catch salamanders, then spending hours trying to get them to race one another. We didn't think anything of the orb and we didn't notice how strangely out of place it was or how oddly it was moving. We weren't even thinking about it when we stopped to prepare supper on the fire.

As Mike muddled together tin-can chili using the fire irons atop smooth stones encircling our smokeless fuel source, I grabbed a flat skip stone from gravel and sent it leaping across the lake in shimmering ripples. It lasted a couple of heartbeats before it sank. Nothing seemed wrong as all of this was going on and we ate in silence, enjoying the peace. For a little while, I think we forgot about the scary paranormal legends and were just enjoying the peace and quiet. Honestly though, I still felt like we were eerily secluded and isolated out there.

Vulnerable was the word that kept running through my head but I didn't dare say that. I didn't want to spoil the fun for my best friend and also, it was a self-preservation mechanism. I didn't want him to tease me. When we thought there were enough stars out in the sky for easier night fishing, we re-baited our rods and cast deeper out. Yet despite bobbers twitching sporadically, we didn't manage to catch anything over the course of the next hour or so. At last, I reeled my line fully in and checked the plastic frog lure with mild frustration only to find its rubber mangled by small incisors. Mike examined the mauled lure, raising his eyebrows. He mentioned something about otters playing with lines and the bites being something more than just play bites. But then he shrugged it off and it seemed like he was talking more to himself than to me anyway so I didn't respond or say anything to him about it. The way it looked though made me terribly nervous. Mike was right. Those hadn't been play bites from otters and the fish don't have teeth like that. So, what was in the water that had chewed my lure up like that? I tried not to think about it but I was once again instinctively scared and this time it wasn't just going away. I felt panicked and like we were suddenly and all at once in imminent danger. From what, I didn't know but I was as sure of it as I was of my own name. As I dug in my tackle box for a replacement, I suddenly had an intense urge from mother nature and I told Mike I would be back in a minute. I hurried off to the outskirts of our camp to relieve myself as he shrugged in response and tossed me a flashlight. sudden urgent nature called.

Mike jokingly called out that I needed to watch out for the fish monster and I gave him the finger in response. We both laughed but inside I wasn't laughing at all. I was scared. Chiding myself for being so silly, I shuffled cautiously into the first border of brush seeking decent concealment, sweeping the harsh LED glow over all of the tangled shadows. It took several long and anxious minutes before the urge allowed itself relief. I hastily got myself together and finished up, trying to get my anxiety to stop rising before I went back to where Mike was waiting for me. Just as I was about to head back to the lake, I heard something very large rustling around in the bushes behind me. I froze, listening intently and trying to figure out what kind of animal it could have been. It sounded huge, whatever it was. I didn't want to panic, but I was panicking anyway. I was about twenty feet from the lake and the noises were about twenty feet behind me. I had to strain my ears in order to hear more. I saw Mike coming towards me. I put my finger to my mouth to shush him as I scanned the treeline with the flashlight. He told me he heard it too and thought it was me. We were whispering and he said that he thought I had gotten stuck in some brambles and was making sure I was okay. Obviously that was a lie and he was either freaked out by the lake all alone or he felt the same thing I was feeling; that there was something out there with us, and that it was hungry and malevolent. I don't know where those feelings came from except to say that they were there and they were strong. We tried to be as silent as possible and as we looked around we saw that there was something that didn't belong in the bushes ahead of us but it seemed to be shrinking away from the brightness of the LED flashlight. I turned it off and we were in almost total darkness, with only the dim crescent moon and the twinkling stars to show us anything. Then, it stepped out from its hiding spot and revealed itself. It was a moment I would never forget and it still gives me nightmares. What happened next is what makes me question my reality and reality in general constantly.

Suddenly everything was quiet and I think we noticed the silence before the massive creature before us registered. We were momentarily distracted by splashing coming from the lake and we turned around and saw another one of the creatures that stood before us in the darkness. We could only see it in shadow but knew it would be the death of us if we didn't think fast and get the hell out of there. Against my better judgment I walked forwards several steps, taking a huge chance in approaching the creature. Against my better judgment, I allowed my morbid curiosity to draw me forward. I crept out slowly seeking the real form behind the shadowy shape. It was huge, at least seven feet wide and seven feet tall. It was incredibly muscular and I heard Mike behind me whispering frantically that we needed to get out of there. The beast stepped forward and Mike shined the light on it. It growled and roared and before it turned and ambled slowly back into the wilderness, we saw what it really was. The one behind us wasn't anywhere to be seen and we were nervous about that too. The creature's low, hairy form loped swiftly along the ground and we turned to run. That's when we saw the other one. It was just standing at the edge of the lake. It was vaguely bipedal, like the other one but a little different. This one was thinner, but just as muscular and was only about five feet tall and maybe a few inches. It was hunched and it had something akin to spikes all along its back that reminded me, somewhat hilariously or maybe deliriously, of a triceratops dinosaur and its face looked reptilian as well. It snarled and showed its muscles to us. It was as though it were getting into a fighting stance and readying itself for an attack. It had very large lips. They were almost comically large and bright pink, its nose almost non-existent. Its eyes were completely black and it stuck its tongue out as it loudly hissed. We just wanted to get out of there and had to come into close proximity to that fish monster in order to get to the Jeep. We had no intention of collecting any of our belongings but we stood there, frozen and knowing there were more of them out there. They could have been anywhere and we were completely and totally unprepared for an attack. How can you prepare yourself to defend against something that you couldn't possibly fathom ever existed? It was paranormal- supernatural. Then, suddenly and without warning, it leaned forward and let out an earth shaking growl that made the weather ripple behind and under him. He turned and dove into the lake and disappeared. We booked it out of there and never looked back.

The whole ride home we were in a panic and Mike almost drove us off the road several times. It took us so long to get out of there and the whole time I kept thinking I saw those strange monsters lurking in every single shadow in those woods. They were behind every tree and for weeks they were all I could see. I was in shock, but too afraid of what people would think to go and try to get help. Mike was never the same and that's something else and a whole other story completely. Nowadays I search for and seek out the paranormal and do as much research as possible. My wife helps me and we sort of do it as a hobby. We haven't yet gone back to face the fish monsters and we also haven't faced the horrific beast she encountered, also while at a lake in the woods in her hometown. I don't know what else to call the thing we saw that night but I still see it in my night-mares and sometimes, when I'm all alone, I think I see it lurking in the shadows in the corner of my bedroom. I know it's impossible that it would be there but I think that's a part of the trauma and I've recently come to believe that only by going back and facing my fears will I truly ever be free of the terror that boils up and then over, inside of me, randomly and all the time. My wife also wants to write her story down so she will send hers in and when we go back to that secluded lake and that same isolated area to camp, I'll let you know what happens with the creatures. I'm not going to leave until I find them. I've investigated so many other places and have come up against and spotted so many other horrific and demonic things, that there's nothing that could ever phase me anymore. Never mock the things you don't understand, even if you don't believe in them because I think Mike and I would have been more alert if we hadn't been so arrogant as to think that human beings are the most intelligent creatures out there. Anyway, that's all for now. Thanks again.

———

If you enjoyed this book, check out Erik Lake's other books on Amazon.

# ABOUT THE AUTHOR

Erik Lake, a pen name adopted to maintain privacy, is a seasoned author with a deeply-rooted passion for the mysteries of human culture and the unexplained. Prior to embarking on his writing career, he served as a professor of anthropology at a prestigious university, where he was celebrated for his captivating lectures and scholarly publications. His academic pursuits led him across the globe, from the jungles of the Amazon to the mountainous terrains of the Himalayas, in search of understanding the complexities of human behavior and tradition.

Throughout his academic tenure, Erik developed a keen interest in folklore, myths, and the stories that often go untold or are overshadowed by mainstream narratives. It was this curiosity that led him to explore themes of the paranormal and the enigmatic phenomena that challenge our understanding of reality.

Since leaving academia, Erik has devoted himself to full-time writing, specializing in works that merge his anthropological background with topics often considered too taboo or unsettling for conventional scholarly dialogue.

Erik Lake brings to the literary world a rare blend of academic rigor and open-minded curiosity. Whether he's shedding light on cryptids, spirits, or age-old legends, his works provide a well-balanced blend of skepticism and wonder, prompting readers to question their own beliefs and perspectives.

Away from the pen and paper, Erik enjoys hiking, amateur photography, and spending time with his family in a quaint, undisclosed location surrounded by nature's untamed beauty. Yet, the woods for him are not just a retreat but an ongoing field of research—a labyrinth of endless questions and bewildering phenomena that continue to fuel his prolific writing career.

## ALSO BY ERIK LAKE

## ALSO BY FREE REIGN PUBLISHING